Y0-BCS-567

AFRICAN WRITERS SERIES

FOUNDING EDITOR Chinua Achebe

Susanne Mamdani

Nairobi Dec 1984.

THE OUTCASTS

Bonnie Lubega

HEINEMANN EDUCATIONAL BOOKS
London · Ibadan · Nairobi

Heinemann Educational Books
22 Bedford Square, London WC1B 3HH
PMB 5205 Ibadan POB 45314 Nairobi
EDINBURGH · MELBOURNE · AUCKLAND
HONG KONG · SINGAPORE · NEW DELHI · KUALA LUMPUR
KINGSTON · EXETER (NH) · PORT OF SPAIN

ISBN 0 435 90105 2

© Bonnie Lubega 1971
First published 1971
Reprinted 1980

TO
*The 'fertilizers' of East Africa's
so-called literary desert.*

Set, printed and bound in Great Britain by
Fakenham Press Limited, Fakenham, Norfolk

ONE

IT was just dawning. The amber sky was gently undressing out of the dark mantle to the melodious music of a host of birds. Bare-breasted and lanky, the lonely early-riser stood in front of his scantily thatched grass-and-wattle hut. He was staring at the clouds dressing themselves in all the colours of the hidden sun.

The old piece of calico which dangled around his loins had never been washed since he bought it from the Indian dukawallah over a year ago. As he stretched first one arm and then the other, all his limbs crackled as if his bones were pieces of dry burning firewood.

He yawned for six long seconds, his mouth and nostrils shooting out a hot steam from deep down in his well-filled lungs. Thoughtfully he watched the steam evaporating in the cold air of the morning and disappearing from view. In the process he wiped off, with his middle finger, the two grains of tears which had accompanied the yawn.

In one corner of his enclosure some smoke climbed lazily in timid coils as if it was afraid of the biting cold. He had made the fire the previous night, and had heaped plenty of dried cattle dung on to it so that the fire should burn throughout the night. The rising smoke mingled with the piquant steam from the constant urine and the fuming, flabby dung excreted by the herd of lowing cattle.

He sniffed in the acrid air; breathed in deeply. For him it was the normal thing to do. He had been born and

I

bred in this kind of atmosphere. In fact he had become part of it.

His heart had grown with the love of sharing life with cattle – the precious ones. For him there was nothing so exciting, nothing so lovable, nothing so beautiful in the world as living with cattle. Dreaming about them; feeling their very pulses beating. Talking to them, and through a curious kind of telepathy, putting his inner messages across into their minds. His very soul, like the soul of a gigantic ghost, moved about with each animal in the herd, embracingly, caressingly.

The cattle, too, knew him. They could smell him from a long distance. In their silent language they told each other not to worry about their enemies. He was always around. He would protect them. Whenever they thought of him, the cattle made sporadic moos as if to confirm their good opinion of him.

All around his kraal there was nothing but a stretch of wild bush. Beyond this was a strip of thick forest which ran along a marsh where he always watered the cattle. This forest was the home of many kinds of wild beasts, both ferocious ones and harmless ones. On the other side of the rough bush that surrounded his kraal was a beautiful emerald sea of coffee fields, vast banana plantations and green vegetables. All spreading out and away as if to avoid his uninviting surroundings.

This was the most beautiful and nestling village which he always admired but could not live in.

Kayonga village abounded with a kind of civilization which was far too different from the life which surrounded him. His black masters and their multitudes of relatives occupied every inch of its soil, their sanctum.

The occupants of Kayonga village were almost unaware of his existence. It was only when they spoke about their cattle, which he looked after, that they remembered there was a human being. A human being who wrapped his soul around their cattle.

It was only when he happened to pass through this sprawling village to fetch the cattle salt from their homes, his lungs would share the sweet air they breathed. Only then would the people he worked for remember his name, ask after their cattle, greet him.

'Karekyezi, how are the cows . . .? How are the calves . . . ? Do they eat a lot of grass? . . . and how are you . . . how's your wife Kabahuma?'

Nobody cared whether there were children in his kraal or not. Apart from going into that village and meeting its people, Karekyezi's only and immediate human neighbours were the members of his household. His wife, his younger brothers, sisters and children, all crammed into that small hut.

Then he had nocturnal visitors who often came to keep him and his household company; to stir the monotony of his kraal life. The laughing hyenas, the yelping jackals, the growling wildcats. A host of them. Now and then a prowling leopard would sneak around the enclosure and threaten the cattle. By his sharp instinct Karekyezi would sense the trouble, call out his households, and watch over the cattle. It was only a few days before, when his instincts had given way to a deep slumber, that a lion attacked the kraal and killed a fat heifer . . .

Owls, too, pestered him. They perched themselves nightly on his enclosure, breaking the stillness of the night. They hooted, now in unison, now one after another, as if they were a band of musicians he had employed to entertain his family and the cattle.

'Howit-whoooo,' they kept changing the dull note.

Karekyezi cast another glance at the sky, now bathing fast in the sun's rays. He sniffed, approved of the pungent smell with a nod of his shaggy head, then he stooped and

3

grabbed the neatly-halved gourd that lay by the side of the ever-open entrance to his hut. Barefooted, he waded through the boggy cattle dung, patting each animal affectionately, calling it fondly by name.

'Ugh, ugh, ugh Kaasa . . . ugh, ugh, ugh Rujumba . .'

It was as if he was singing to each of them, his soul penetrating theirs with the fondness of a mother. He felt his way slowly until he reached the other end of the enclosure and stood by the glowing fire. Each animal he had patted got up on all fours and politely wished him a good morning.

'Mooooooooo-ing,' it said.

Karekyezi was doing the routine check he carried out early every morning to make sure the cattle were all there and safe. Now he spread his free hand towards the fire and rubbed its warmth into his cheeks. Then he turned to fondle the cows. At that moment Kaasa started to urinate in front of him. Karekyezi promptly held his gourd behind her and caught the urine until the container was full. Then he cupped his palm, scooped the warm urine, and washed his face. Ahhhhh . . . it was quite refreshing in the cold morning air. With the same warm urine he washed his mouth, gurgled, and spat. He repeated the process, squirting out jets until he was satisfied his mouth was now clean, fresh. He heaved hot air from his lungs, smiled to himself, and tipped away the dregs that had remained at the bottom of the gourd.

'Ugh, ugh, ugh Kaasa, there's nothing filthy about you,' he told her fondly, 'you're next to my mother. All of you are my mothers. Beautiful, gentle, good, clean. Your urine tastes as sweet as honey in my mouth . . .'

All the cows moo'd. Karekyezi surveyed them proudly, and stroked those in his way as he traced his steps back to the hut. He put the gourd back in its place for the other households to use in the same manner.

Once again he looked up at the now bright sky and

4

nodded his head in affirmative as if the cows had asked him a question. He made another long yawn, his throat gurgling in a package of air. Then he walked to the stockade-gate of the enclosure.

The cattle were watching him. Kicking their legs impatiently. Mooing hopefully. Swinging their tails from side to side, smacking the irritating flies in the process. Dropping mounds of fresh dung; pouring forth streams of urine. All set for a dash out into the fresh air. When he flung the gate open they stampeded madly to it. Squeezing each other's ribs. Their horns clapping like spearsmen's weapons in a furious battle. They almost tore the gate apart, each was anxious to have a full glimpse of the new day.

Karekyezi stood aside and watched them with mixed feelings. Of course he was very fond of them, nay, he really loved them. But his employers had disturbed his mind. They were mean towards him after all that he had suffered on account of their cattle. It was true, he knew, they would never pay him in money. It was also true that they gave him some food whenever Kabahuma went to beg for it in the village. It was perfectly true he was drinking their milk freely as his terms of employment. But why did they want to sack him; as if, instead of grazing their cattle on good grass, he was feeding them on his own shit? Why? But wait . . . he would show these employers that he was not so stupid as they thought him to be. In fact they would envy him one day . . . With that thought Karekyezi grinned broadly, as he watched the cattle pouring themselves into the *saazi*, kraal courtyard. There the animals would stop and wait for him. He had disciplined them into this habit and they would never move an inch until he ordered them with a gentle touch of his stick.

He walked straight back into his hut, took his long clay pipe from the side of the fireplace and filled it with tobacco. He knocked a glowing cinder off a burning log, fished it out with his fingers, and placed it on the pipe. Then he squatted by the fire, spreading his legs wide apart to let its warmth reach freely to his naked genitals. Then he began to smoke, silently, thoughtfully – and with relish.

All around him snores were still roaring from the beds of his households. Yes, the beds; heaps of dried grass on which the family clustered themselves like a litter of young rabbits in a burrow. They slept on goat, sheep or calfskins. They covered themselves with age-old blankets, many of which were the women's dresses during the day.

On Karekyezi's bed Kabahuma lay on the same old calfskin which his mother had presented to the couple the day they married. Kabahuma was then fourteen. It was the same skin which had replaced the one on which his father first slept with Kabahuma on their wedding day before Karekyezi could claim her as wife. Customs had to be adhered to. His father had to enjoy the young bride to make sure she was worthy of the dowry of twenty healthy cows that he had paid for his son; that Kabahuma was still a virgin.

Karekyezi's father had, on several occasions, visited Kabahuma's father's kraal. Sometimes it was to discuss where to find new pastures, at other times it was just to get together socially and drink. He had always seen the girl and on one such occasion had joked to her father.

'Here's a beautiful bride for my son. Name your price, Father . . .'

Her father had then burst out into hearty laughter, his daughter shyly hiding her face, and said:

'You're a rich man, Father. You can, of course, afford to pay twenty cows for such a beautiful calf?'

'You have them,' Karekyezi's father had replied with a boisterous laugh, gulping more beer.

From what had been a joke on that day, matters had then come to a head; had been thought of seriously on both

6

sides. All the marriage preliminaries had been gone into. Kabahuma's aunts and uncles had met and discussed the idea, and had finally given their consent. Karekyezi's father had then been asked to introduce the boy.

The boy was then sixteen. Slim, roughly strong, handsome. For the visit he had been dressed in a clean, two-piece calico. The loin piece, and the cloak, which he knotted on his upper left shoulder to allow it to dangle freely over his chest and back. The loin piece he had securely wound around his waist and had used a dry banana bark for the belt. As a symbol of his manhood, Karekyezi had held a long, razor-sharp, shining spear and his cattle-driving stick in his right hand, and a long, clay tobacco pipe in his left hand. To complete the picture of a decently-dressed man, he had strapped his feet in sandals cut out of a lorry-tyre. His father had been attired in a similar way.

They had been met outside the kraal by a group of men and women. Kabahuma was holding a wooden container full of milk, fresh and unboiled. This she had offered to her suitor who had to drink the milk while standing and in one draught.

Karekyezi had been struck by Kabahuma's beauty. She was slim, with big bright eyes; the eyes of a pregnant cow. Her nose was small. Her graceful neck was decorated with beads and wire necklaces. He could see that her body, wrapped up in a new blanket, was beautifully shaped. More coils of wire rings were shining on her ankles. His smile had tickled hers. When he stretched his arm to hand over the empty gourd, she gently reached for it with both hands. This, then, had shown Karekyezi Kabahuma's shapely fingers with their ivory-white nails. In short, her beauty had captivated him instantly.

She had shyly flitted another enchanting smile, then dashed back into the kraal where her father and other older people were waiting for the guests. Skins had already been spread over the cow-dung floor of the hut and food was cooking on the fire. Her father had noticed her excitement.

'How's the boy,' he had asked her, 'you like him?'

'Eeee, Father,' she had nodded laughingly, 'he's handsome, hihihihi . . .'

Her reply had sealed her future. Karekyezi had not seen her again until shortly before the guests left. Kabahuma and some other girls had hidden themselves behind an old hanging blanket all the time, stealing peeps at him through its holes. They had seen the way he ate his food and the way he drank his beer. A real man, they had secretly commented. Then as she waited for the wedding day, her mother and aunts had once again gathered to give her the final lessons on the aspects of her marriage.

Her future father-in-law would be the first man in her life to test her virginity. This had frightened her. The old man had always appeared sinewy and rough; how could she give herself to such an old man? But her aunts had insisted. What he would do with her would be just for a passing moment.

'Just for a short time,' they had told her, 'and if that short time proves you are still complete, you will get presents. One cow from him and another from your father . . .'

Kabahuma had concealed her fears and then on the wedding day Karekyezi's father had excitedly and forcibly thrust his wildly hungry thing into her, and had almost knocked the young bride out of her senses. A thousand needles had pricked her whole body, and young Kabahuma had stifled a sharp cry. Then as if to soothe her the old man had tried to speak to her.

'Aiiii, my daughter . . . the blood is warm . . . hot, hot, hot . . . auuuuu . . . excellent . . . let them . . . let them take the cows . . . don't cry child . . . a calf for you . . .

8

more, more . . . just a little more . . . only a little . . .
aaaaah . . . let the cows please your people . . . you'll be a
good wife for my son . . .'

The old man had allowed Karekyezi to take posses-
sion of his bride soon after the accomplishment of his own
compensation. Karekyezi's mother had bathed Kabahuma
with a lot of herbs, and afterwards the calfskin on which
she had lain with the old man had been folded and sent to
her parents to prove her virginity. Since then Kabahuma
had taken good care of the second skin, rubbing it with
butter once in a while to keep it soft . . .

'Yes, I must leave before they throw me out,'
Karekyezi mused as he puffed his pipe, spitting jets of
saliva into the hot ashes in the fireplace. 'Let them get
another herdsman, I don't care. And if they think they'll
treat that one better I'll return into my mother's stomach.'
Then loudly he spat his employers as if they were rolled
into his spittle, 'Pthooooh, these ungrateful creatures. They
only think of their cattle and of themselves as if no other
human beings existed in the world. Now they want to kick
me out of the job for nothing! The fools . . . I'll leave
before they do it. I'll retire . . .'

Retire? Well, isn't that what people say after labouring for years if they want to avoid being sacked?
Karekyezi's retirement however, would mean going back
into the same work again. He would start, but in a different
way; a rich man's way of life, he called it.

He had long desired to be his own master. He would
then forget all these years of serfdom, working for the
people who never even thought of him as a person. The
people he had served ever since he was a small boy. What
was the use of being trampled down and fed on the left-
overs?

Karekyezi was forty years old. See the children he
had worked out of Kabahuma! Why should he continue to

9

be a perpetual underdog? He had worked from one employer to another; he had moved around the country from one village to another; he had roamed the bush tenderly grazing their cattle as if the animals were his own brothers and sisters, but he had not come across a good master.

'The whole bunch of them has always been the same,' Karekyezi had told his households. 'Only a few, a very few times in my life have I met some considerate masters. But even then, they were selfish and discriminating. Some of them were real fools, brainless. I had to quit the job before they found out what I was doing to them. You must keep up our secret when you grow up because that is the only way you'll survive and profit from these brainless people . .'

The secret was effective and had been handed down over a number of years. From it Karekyezi, like his other cousins, had built up his own large stock of cattle he kept elsewhere among his relatives. He had always stolen newly-born calves without his employers even suspecting it. It was easy for him to trick his employers whenever he wanted to steal their calves. After all, didn't they come only rarely to his kraal to see their cattle? Didn't they come only when he had told them their cows had calved? Were they not afraid of soiling their feet with the cow dung that lay everywhere around his kraal?

'I'll show these fools that a *mulaalo*, kraal-dweller, can be cleverer and richer than a *munnakyalo*, village-dweller,' Karekyezi muttered to himself over his pipe, stroking the underside of his thighs which were almost roasting from the heat of the fire. 'They're just a bunch of stupid cattle owners who can't even use their heads properly.'

He remembered the lion incident in which his whole household had narrowly escaped death. For whose sake would the family have perished? Would not the cattle owners have come the following day to collect their cattle, whisking them away without even feeling compassion for the destroyed family? When the kraal women raised wild alarms and ear-splitting ululations calling for help, did anybody come from the village? Was it not Karekyezi himself and his boys alone who killed that lion? . . .

'Pthooooh,' he spat and swore, '*kaate rubura,* confound them,' then he bared his teeth, biting the top lip with the lower teeth, and cursed, 'ahiiiiiima, to hell!'

TWO

KABAHUMA was not really asleep; she was merely resting. She always needed such rest whenever her husband screwed her long and proper. However, this morning Karekyezi had jumped off her quickly before he went out to check on the cattle. Now she lay quiet, only turning herself occasionally, coughing and chewing her spittle. From the fireside where he sat Karekyezi heard her and called.

'Bride-of-mine,' he said, 'the day outside already opens its eyes'.

'Eeeeh,' she replied, turned heavily, heaved a deep sigh and yawned audibly, at the same time mumbling words to the effect of 'wake them all.'

Kabahuma knew exactly what she was expected to do along with the other womenfolk – to open the new day by sweeping the boggy cattle dung and heap it at the usual place outside the kraal. In the few months the family had lived in this place the heap had turned into a growing hillock. This hillock owed its growth not only to the freshly added cattle dung, but also to the family's daily contribution of emptying their bowels on it. However, this hillock had another very important use awaiting it. The family had had a similar hillock in their previous place before they came to settle here. The characteristics surrounding these hillocks had been the same for generations. When Karekyezi's mother had died a few months ago, the family had had a ready tomb awaiting her remains. They placed the body, squatting and naked, right inside the hillock, cemented the grave properly with the dung and had forthwith emigrated to the new, safe place. They had to leave immediately lest the death which had taken the old lady claimed another member of the family. Tradition dictated that the safest way to hide from this cruel death was to leave the surroundings immediately after the burial . . .

Thus, they had hurriedly gathered their scanty belongings, packed them in old skins and blankets, and had left the place immediately. Some of Karekyezi's kinsmen had come to attend his mother's burial and to help the family move out; while the adults carried heavier things on their heads, the children carried all the empty wooden milk containers – calabashes and gourds.

Since he knew every part of this ridge, Karekyezi had had some of the uncultivated areas earmarked, just in case anything should happen to force the family out of their present settlement. There were always many unforseeable things which could happen suddenly; a landowner might need that particular part of his land for growing his crops, and without warning he could throw out the kraal-family just like that! Another reason was that owls were the confirmed emmissaries of death. Some ignorant people said that owls loved to perch themselves on kraal-enclosures because cattle dung attracted them. But Karekyezi and Kabahuma had long known that once the number of these birds of prey increased, and their hoots grew louder and more frequent, that was the unmistakable sign of danger. Any member of the family might suddenly drop dead.

There were hosts of reasons which had prompted Karekyezi to earmark a number of places and to be constantly on the look-out for more open bush on the ridge. Jackals were another sign of danger. Once they started howling around the kraal that was a sure sign of an epidemic. The kraal would be attacked by plague. Other wild beasts did not terrify the family. These they could always fight and kill with their sharp spears.

So, the first thing to do in the new place had been to build the new home. Karekyezi had assigned two of the big boys to drive the cattle into the pastures while he and the rest of his kinsmen had immediately started the work of erecting the kraal. First they had built the family hut and then another smaller hut opposite to house the calves. This done, they had collected a lot of dry branches of all kinds of thorny trees. With these they had built a strong enclosure around the two huts, thus providing a wide enough space in the centre for the cattle. Kabahuma and her female group had cut a lot of grass, some of it for thatching the huts and the rest for the family beds.

By the time the cattle had returned in the evening the whole work had been completed, and a good fire was crackling in a corner of the space reserved for the cattle. Kabahuma had also made a quick visit to the nearest house in the village to beg for food.

And so the new life had begun, and the cattle-owners had been informed of the new settlement. It was important to inform them; not that cattle-owners cared a bit to know the reasons for this sudden emigration; their sole concern was to know the whereabouts of their animals. The cattle, rather than the herdsmen, had to be kept under observation. Otherwise all the villages from ridge to ridge; the whole district; the whole county would raise hell. Moreover, each cattle-owner, by knowing the settlement, could make sure of the daily flow of his share of milk . . .

When Kabahuma got out of the bed one of the boys handed her some warm urine in the same gourd Karekyezi had used. The rest of the family had washed their faces in the *saazi* where the cattle stood. And now it was Kabahuma's turn as she was the last to get up. She sat on the threshold and washed her face. She used her index finger to wash her teeth, gargled and spat. She splashed some of the urine on her fat arms, to erase the scratches which she had made with her long nails during sleep. With the rest of the urine she washed her feet, skipping the ankles which were laden with wire rings, and then washed her legs up to the knee.

In the meantime Karekyezi and the boys filed out to the *saazi* to milk the cows. With an almost inborn expertise, each sat on his haunches, holding *ekyanzi*, wooden milk-container, between the knees, and stroked, tickled and pulled at the cows' teats which squirted jets of milk.

Kagabu, the youngest brother, had perhaps wrongly manipulated the cow he was milking. For suddenly she turned an angle and gave him a kick. He fell backwards and all the milk spilled over his face and chest, and soaked through his calico, sticking it to his body.

The cow seemed contented with her revenge. For she looked back at him with her big, wide-open eyes and moo'd an approval. None of Kagabu's colleagues helped him. All junior members of the clan were supposed to learn, expected to know how to handle milch cows.

'Pthoooh!' Kagabu spat and swore irritably behind milk-painted face, '*nyabura nyowe, kaate rubura*. To hell with them all, the owners and their cows. I graze the beasts and what do I get? Kicks and kicks and kicks. The owners sit comfortably filling their stomachs with *matooke* and wait for their milk. Ahiiiiiima *kaate rubura*, pthooooh.'

His young colleagues laughed at his bitterness.

'They're still your employers, don't forget that,' Karekyezi reminded him, 'and they'll always be your masters until you get enough brains to make yourself independent. When you build up your own stock then you can shake off their employment. But without that you'll die their slave . . .'

15

No more was said. With the exception of sporadic moos the only other sound was from the milk squirting into the wooden containers. Kagabu returned to his cow, nervously working the milk into his *ekyanzi*, starting every time the cow made a slight turn.

'You must learn how to handle the cows,' Karekyezi rebuked him. 'When are you going to be a man? Are you going to wait until you prove it with your penis into your bride? At your age I was already tough. When I married Kabahuma I was like a lion. Ask her how she felt my power . . .'

'Yes, but this cow is impossible. She doesn't like being milked . . .' Kagabu replied.

'Lies. There's no cow that's impossible. Stroke her udder gently, then the teats, and milk. Must I always teach you that? Suppose I'm not at your marriage to teach you how to fuck your bride, will you simply lie there and look at her? Use your head. Cows are like our women. Stroke them, tickle them and then work on them . . .'

Kagabu kept quiet. He did not like to argue with Karekyezi over things he had no idea of. He had no experience with women. How would he know that a man first had to be gentle to a woman, even if it was his own wife? How would he know that a man first had to stroke, then tickle and finally give his wife the works?

Karekyezi's remark, however, amused the other bigger boys. For they burst out laughing like the over-inflated dried bladder of a cow which children in the village often used as a football. The other boys' laughter encouraged Karekyezi who now rocked with laughter like them.

'Yes,' he said, 'it's true. Ask them. Ask all the women. Be men yourselves. Show them your manhood. Excite them first and then . . . even if it means breaking their backs . . . do it. They like it that way. First gentle and then rough . . .'

After more laughter had died down, Barigye, the older boy asked:

'Why be gentle first and then rough?'

'Don't be stupid,' Karekyezi rebuked amusedly, 'you know our proverb and answer me, "When outside of the kraal?"'

'A hyena dances and shits,' Barigye answered.

'And once inside the kraal?'

'His salivas flow and he bites.'

'And do you know the reason why he dances and shits when he is outside?' Karekyezi asked further.

'Yes, because he hasn't got what he wants yet,' Barigye gave a prompt answer.

'Then you know the rest,' Karekyezi went oh, 'don't ask me silly questions again.'

This conversation did not stop the progress of milking the cows. However, Kagabu had found it so captivating that he had somehow stopped milking his cow and had glued his eyes on Karekyezi interestedly. It was after he had made his last remark that Karekyezi, on impulse, turned towards Kagabu. Then he barked at him.

'Am I a woman,' he said, 'that you have to stare at me so soulfully? This boy is going to be useless, I tell you, Barigye. I'm not sure if he will not forget his duty with his wife and go on ogling at . . .'

Karekyezi's last remark was drowned in a fresh out-burst of laughter from the boys. At the same time the cattle started lowing impatiently, swinging their tails from side to side to fend off the flies. Kagabu obediently turned his attention to his work as the laughter from the others died down.

At last all the containers were filled and lined up in the usual place; a cool corner inside the hut. Kabahuma

17

covered most of them with a hard, neatly knitted cap, and left the rest for immediate consumption. Both the adults and the children hungrily drank the unboiled milk, passing *ekyanzi* from mouth to mouth. Along with the milk they ate cold slices of cassava which Kabahuma had roasted under hot ashes the night before.

Karekyezi and the boys took out their pipes. At the age of fourteen Kagabu was already a tobacco addict. They wore their lorry-tyre sandals, gathered their spears and sticks, whistled high and low, and sang merrily. Life was astir all around. The women labouring with the flabby cattle dung; the younger, naked children rubbing their eyes; the cattle lowing in the *saazi*.

The sun was now climbing the sky, shining beautifully on the silvery grains of dew which clung to the vegetation. Flies were zooming all over the place and armies o blue-bottles were singing, dancing, and rejoicing on and over the hillock. Others were racing and landing on the naked bodies of the children, eagerly nibbling away the matter in the children's eyes. The children, in turn, were swatting the flies away with their hands. They were looking at things around them with their teeth, as it were, rather than with their sore eyes.

Today was a hot day. As the day advanced towards noon the heat increased. The herdsmen and their cattle roamed the bush wherever they could find good grass. Usually they met other parties in the good rangelands and herded their cattle together. In this way the older men would gather, squat on an ant-hill and talk, leaving the young ones to look after the cattle.

Kagabu felt hungry. He strayed for a moment to look for wild berries and in the process rounded a bush, squatted, and began to open his bowels. Just then he heard a sudden swish-swash in the tall grass not far away from him. Arrested by the sound, that mingled with the rattling from his backside, Kagabu cast a quick glance behind and shouted one word which almost chilled the heat of the day.

'*Injzoka!*'

He jumped clear as a big, lengthy python swiftly made its way towards him, its fierce eyes glued on him, to mesmerize him. Its wide mouth was open, its tongue darting out with hunger and thirst. Kagabu was petrified, he remained rooted but undaunted. When was he going to be a man? The words flashed across his mind.

'Now,' he shouted to himself.

In the twinkling of an eye Kagabu was grappling with the monster. He was in a furious battle; either he or the snake had to die. Such danger as this either gave one wings or courage. There was no time for wings. Courage, boy, courage. Be a man.

The monster was trying to gather his legs with its powerful tail. Kagabu planted his legs apart, using all the strength he had; his spear the only weapon in his hand. With its tail the python coiled itself around his leg, was crushing it. Its head was aiming at his own head. Then, with incredible agility, Kagabu stumbled forth and thrust his spear right into its open mouth; still holding the shaft firmly in both hands he reeled and fell, pinning the monster's head down on the ground. Its tail let go of his leg and flapped hither and thither with pain.

Kagabu was sweating profusely. His legs were covered with his own running shit. When his colleagues arrived they found him still holding the spear, its prey struggling hard. They crushed its head with their sticks and the reptile lay still.

'Now you're a man,' Karekyezi patted him on the shoulder, smiling broadly, 'you've used your head. Take the leaves and clean yourself. You're stinking.'

'What would you do if you were shitting and an

enemy attacked you?' Kagabu asked. 'Would you first look for leaves before you even had the chance to finish?'

They all laughed aloud as he cleaned himself.

'*Kaate rubura*,' they swore simultaneously, pthooooh . . . pthooooh . . . pthoooooh,' each spat on the dead snake.

They left it to rot on its battle-field. Who cared for its skin? Who said its skin was valuable? Who would skin a python, anyway – unless one was a witch and needed the skin to charm other people? Some witches said that if you cut a python-skin into bits, crushed it, and offered it to lepers, it cured them. But who was a leper?

The party moved on and met a number of relatives grazing their own cattle. Most of them had started life, like Karekyezi, as serfs. But through the ingenuity of the 'tradition handed down by our people' these relatives had eventually pensioned themselves off. Now they had formed a co-operative ring, and were keeping their eyes on their kith and kin who were still in the employ of the thoughtless yeomen.

'It's a long time, Karekyezi, since you last sent me a calf,' Rweza mildly rebuked his cousin. 'Are their cows no longer calving these days; or have they become as barren as a rock? What are you doing with the bulls, have they grown too old and powerless . . . ?'

'That's not the point, Rweza,' Karekyezi answered, 'the bulls seem to be too slow these days. Maybe they don't sniff the smell of the cows' holes!'

'Nonsense,' Rweza replied, 'why don't you rub their testicles with all these stimulating herbs we have? Do it and you'll see if their penis's will not become stiff and shoot calves into the cows . . .'

These rich and expert kraalmen had a lot to tell and to advise their employed relatives. They lived deep in the bush with their vast herds of cattle. They hardly passed through Kayonga village. They visited the village only

20

when they brought their butter to barter for food, and a calabash of *mwenge*. They loved the brew, and would drink it until each was completely drunk.

However they needed more of their relatives to go and live with them, to establish a community of their own. Since nobody wanted them in the villages, they had to live somewhere as a people. Those who inhabited the villages called them uncivilized savages, outcasts.

'It won't be long before I join you, Rweza,' Karekyezi broke the news. 'They want to push me out because of the lion which killed one of their heifers; they accuse me of letting the cattle in my kraal go and eat all their sweet-potatoes, beans and maize. I'm tired, Rweza, I must come soon . . .'

'You're quite right, Karekyezi. You have enough cattle now in our kraals. But what's wrong with your staying on for a little while to get more calves during a good season before you come?'

'I have heard, Rweza,' Karekyezi replied after a moment's pause, 'I'll do it. Some of these cows are now pregnant; I'll wait until they deliver. If the chance goes well with me, then expect a few more calves for your kraal. Now I'll leave the boys to take care of the cattle . . .'

'Where are you going?' Rweza asked sharply.

'I'm thirsty, Rweza. They might have something in the village. I'll go and see . . .'

THREE

KABAHUMA and her team finished their only chore of sweeping the kraal. Now there was nothing else left for them to do except laze under the sun. Kabahuma had already sent some of the older girls to take the milk into the village to those owners whose cows were providing it. The women never thought of doing anything else. For them to dig even a small piece of land around them to grow the family's food was unknown, unheard of, unthinkable.

'After all,' Kabahuma would tell her companions, 'why bother to break our backs when we may have to move somewhere else at any time? Isn't my husband always changing his job? How do we know that we're not going to go to another village soon? And leave all our strength behind, after breaking our backs . . .?'

But it was not so much a matter of breaking their backs, as the fact that they had never touched a hoe in their entire lives. When the men left for the pastures the women always spent their day drinking large amounts of milk. They basked under the warm sun after smearing their bodies with gallons of crude butter; they slept and gossiped. On other days they invaded Kayonga village to beg for food.

Kabahuma however, was a kind-hearted woman. She loved children, and made friends with the village mothers who needed her butter which was her main exchange for their food. Of course she was a stranger to them and would always remain an uncivilized stranger, but they needed her butter to add the taste to their food. A good cook always made a good wife, and butter improved that cooking.

When Lozio's children arrived for their milk, Kabahuma was basking in the nude outside the kraal by the *saazi*. She sat carelessly and was busy exploring in her clothes for those uncomfortable little parasites which sucked heavily on her blood. They always annoyed her, sweetly tickling her all over the body; compelling her to scratch herself leaving long and deep lines.

Now she was arresting them; prosecuting them; passing her judgement on them. Condemning to death and executing those lice between her thumb-nails. As she squeezed the lice to death, mercilessly bursting them with a little 'click', the two village boys stopped. They watched silently, mouths agape. They looked at each other, pulled faces, then turned their heads and spat on the grass. Her stark naked children, besmeared with streaks of cow dung, were playing hide-and-seek near the hillock.

'Mine-Kabahuma,' the older boy called with that prefix expressing politeness, 'my mother has sent us for our milk.'

Kabahuma was taken aback. She lifted her eyes from her work of execution, saw the children, and began to collect herself majestically, unconcerned as it were. She pulled on the clothes to cover her massive naked body, then she spoke to them.

'Go, my children,' she said, 'go into the house or play with your friends. I'm coming now . . .'

But the little friends on the hillock eyed the new-comers as complete strangers. And the newcomers twitched their noses, shunning the smell around them. They, too, eyed Kabahuma's children curiously. Things seemed strange around here, they thought. There was a moment's suspense between the two young parties, each side keeping aloof. Then Mama Kabahuma propelled herself inside the kraal and into the hut which seemed to hang on her back. The two boys followed.

Even when Kabahuma deported herself into the village it was always a sight to see. She wrapped herself in a number of blankets and clothes which she tucked neatly and tied securely round her projecting, swinging posterior, just a ton of fat. Her arms looked like some adult's thighs grafted on to her trunk; her heavy trudge was always calculated. She was a self-propelling cargo of flesh. A long, never-washed piece of calico draped from her half-covered head, reached down to her ankles, hemming in the volume of blankets which wrapped up the cargo.

Her face still bore the features of the beauty she had been before she emulated the size of a cow-elephant. Her small hamitic nose; her big white eyes, still enchanting; her sweet, warm, captivating smile; her ivory-white teeth. It was only the odour which ensued from her daily-buttered, rarely-bathed body which carried another kind of message. The message of the smell of last year's perspiration and decaying cheese. A smell which would make anybody's bowels turn with a rumble; a smell which provoked a stream of salty saliva inside the mouth; foul, rancid.

'Come, my bride's children,' she called Tereza's boys.

In the meantime she grabbed a half-full *ekyanzi* of milk which had been left over by her children. She placed it in front of the two boys and told them to drink it.

'Kill the hunger, my children,' she said.

Then she turned to fill the kettle they had brought. Just then all her children filled the passage to see how village children drank milk. Or did the village children know at all how to drink milk like the kraal children?

The two boys looked at each other, then at the

24

wooden container. The elder whispered something into his brother's ear.

'Don't touch it,' he said, 'it's dirty.'

'Her nails are full of blood,' the younger boy whispered back, 'I don't want to vomit.'

'Drink, children-of-my-lord, drink. Milk is good for children,' she urged them fondly.

'No, we are not hungry. We don't like it,' they refused flatly, stubbornly.

'Then take to my bride this little butter also,' Kabahuma said softly after she had filled their kettle and handed it over to them. 'See her for me and tell her I'll come for some food, you hear my children?'

The two boys did not reply. They merely eyed her as if they had just seen her for the first time. One of them took the kettle and the other carried the small *ensale*, a cut gourd for holding butter. They hurriedly cleared out of the hut, picking their way carefully through the dry patches of the ground. Soon they were out of the kraal, laughing derisively as though the whole place was a lepers' territory.

Their kraal counterparts had followed them to the gate. Straining their sore eyes and 'seeing' through their teeth, the kraal children watched the two scampering figures. Then they burst out laughing, evidently amused by the strange behaviour of the village people. They didn't like the milk? Then why had they come for it?

'Ahiiiiima,' they sang in a chorus, baring their lower teeth and throwing back their heads, 'Ahiiima.'

'Eat your mother's shit,' Lozio's elder son shouted back.

'And her lice,' his younger brother contributed, chewing his jaws as if to show the kraal children how to eat their mother's lice.

Just then the big cargo emerged from behind her children. Apparently Kabahuma had not heard the insults thrown upon her children since she beamed her sweet smile, waved her hand and called out 'See your mother (greetings to your mother).'

The two brats did not even wave back before they disappeared from view.

'Those *balaalo*, kraalmen, are really stupid,' said the older boy shaking his head, 'they live like animals and want us to drink from their containers. Since when did *we*, our people, eat with outcasts?'

'Who told you to call them that?' the younger boy asked.

'Everybody in the village says so.'

'Then I'll tell Mama that Kabahuma was forcing us to drink the milk her children had spat in,' the younger boy replied. 'Maybe Mama will not send us there again.'

Tereza's lunch was just about ready when Kabahuma came sailing up to the kitchen – she stood by the door. She had known how to time the lunches in the village; now she wanted to make her presence felt as she watched Tereza busying herself.

Lozio had brewed *mwenge* on that day and most of his village colleagues were already boozy. Some of them were drinking from gourds. Others were spooning their drink from well-laid banana leaves, arranged on the ground in the form of a small boat. The majority were drinking from banana leaves cleverly folded like a funnel with the lower end closed into a V-joint.

'Mine-*omukyala*, milady,' Kabahuma called, 'are you there?'

'Eeeeh, Kabahuma. Do you appear?' replied Tereza.

'Ehuuu,' Kabahuma sighed heavily, fanned herself, sat down under the eaves, then said, 'I told the children that I was coming. Did they tell you, my bride?'

'They did not say . . . but thank you for my present of butter.'

'Eeeeh, but it was not much, my bride. That was all I had left in the house. Some other day, maybe . . . ehuuuu . . . the children did not say? Sometimes children forget, my bride.' She uncovered her head, fanned herself again, and heaved another deep sigh. 'It's a hot day today. The sun shines so much . . .' she said.

Of course Tereza knew what these remarks implied – Kabahuma wanted something to quench her thirst.

'Do you want some beer, Kabahuma?'

'Eeeeh, my bride . . . thank you . . . thank you so much . . . ayiiii, my bride . . . you have born me.'

Tereza filled a small old gourd, part of its mouth chipped off, and handed it to her unexpected guest. Kabahuma took a long draught, smacked her lips and heaved a sigh. Tereza then asked her to sit under the shade of the banana trees, away from the kitchen, so that Kabahuma's bowel-twisting odour be swept away by the wind towards the plantation.

'You've saved me, my bride,' Kabahuma crooned her thanks as she propelled herself away to the place, 'thank you for always. This terrible heat roasts the throat, my bride . . .'

Food was then served and Kabahuma's was given to her on cooked banana leaves although Tereza had enough plates. Kabahuma did not wash her hands; neither was water given to her for the purpose. After all, were not both the food and the hands hers? Why bother about plates or washing the hands when you were hungry and the food was set before you . . .? With that she attacked her share with a good appetite, dipping morsels of *matooke* into the clay bowl which contained groundnut sauce.

She ate with relish, turning to her gourd from time to time to wash down the tasty food that had been cooked with some of the butter she had presented to Tereza. In no time the leaves were clean of even the smallest crumbs. When her guests had finished eating, Tereza took all the left-overs and dumped them on Kabahuma's cooked leaves.

'Eat more, Kabahuma,' Tereza said, 'and take the rest to your children.'

'You've done well, my bride. You've done your part towards my burial. And when you've finished that butter, send the children, my bride.'

'By the way, Kabahuma,' Tereza asked before the latter raised the question which was now hanging on her lips, 'have you some food for the family?'

'Ayiiii, my bride, it was finished yesterday. I was just about to ask my bride for some . . .'

'All right, I'll give some to you. Send one of the boys in the evening. And take some *mwenge* to your husband, but tell him to bring back my gourd, otherwise when you people come here again you will have nothing to drink from.'

'Ayiiii, maweee, my bride. I've no words to thank you. You have taken them from my mouth . . . now I must go, my bride, before the cattle return . . .'

Tereza replenished the gourd, and handed it to her. Kabahuma collected the little food she had left on the leaves and minutes later was swaggering out of sight. It was by sheer coincidence that on the way home she met her husband returning from the pastures. He was the first to greet her.

'Bride-of-mine, are you there?' As he greeted her his eyes kept glancing at the small gourd which she held in her hands. She answered him by giving him the gourd to have a drink.

'Ahhhhh . . . it's good, really good. From whom?'

'My bride, Tereza,' she replied, without a hint that it had been sent to him, 'they have a lot of it. All the village is gathered there. Are you going?'

'Of course, of course. I'm dying of thirst. I was just wondering if they had it in the village? Lozio is a good man, he'll give me some . . .'

This encouraged Kabahuma to take the gourd away from him before he emptied it. She handed him the children's food to carry and both walked towards the kraal. Karekyezi had to change into clothes which were fit for a visit to the village.

'The boys'll bring in the cattle,' he told her.

But Kabahuma did not need any telling. Whenever her husband decided to leave the cattle in the pastures with the boys, it was always to look for *mwenge*. Once Karekyezi found the drink, he never returned to the pastures that day.

'Eeeeeh,' Kabahuma replied.

FOUR

ONLY the other day Mutwe-gwa-kyalo
had summoned an emergency council. A lion had attacked
one of the kraals which hemmed in Kayonga village and
that kraal happened to be Karekyezi's. Something had to
be done immediately.

'Listen, Fathers,' Mutwe-gwa-kyalo spoke passion-
ately, 'this is a very serious matter. That heifer was a great
loss for our brother Ganaafa. Even if the *balaalo* killed the
beast, the question still remains: why did not this man
Karekyezi build his kraal properly so as to protect our
cattle effectively? Are we going to allow this sort of thing
to happen again?'

Mutwe-gwa-kyalo paused and swept the council with
his searching gaze. A wave of murmurs arose among his
peasant tenant-councillors. But nobody ventured to rise up
and give his views on the matter in hand. Mutwe-gwa-
kyalo might have guessed what was going on among
them.

'Some of you may say it was bad luck. But once a cow
is lost in such circumstances, who is to blame, if not the
mulaalo? And if you still think it was bad luck for Ganaafa,
how was it that the lion chose only Karekyezi's kraal? Is it
not true that it had first surveyed all the kraals and found
that this was the vulnerable one?'

Some of his men nodded their assent. An encourage-
ment to the Chief to go straight to the point.

'We're not going to let this brainless man offer our

cattle to wild beasts like that. He must be sacked, and *now*.'

'You're perfectly right, Father,' supported his deputy amid a thunder of voices. 'This man is hopelessly lazy, I'm not telling lies. Like all his kinsmen, he's careless. Do you remember that it was the cattle which he looks after that broke through the enclosure and ate all Sepiriya's crops?'

'We must have another *mulaalo*. A better one, Fathers. A better one,' Mutwe-gwa-kyalo gnashed his teeth as if he held that 'better one' between them. 'Yes, they're all lazy, but some of them are lazier than the others.'

Buggya had just bought his first cow, and had put it in Karekyezi's kraal. Now he wanted to impress the council about how he felt towards the kraalman.

'This man is already rich, Fathers,' he contributed. 'All he does is take the biggest share of our milk, sell it to the Indians, and get a lot of money to buy his wife tons of blankets to wear . . .'

'That's true,' Solobeza interposed. 'Have I not seen Kabahuma dressed in a new blanket lately? Where did she get it from? Unless she opened her legs to some generous benefactor!'

'Oh, oh, oh,' the whole council exclaimed, roaring with laughter.

'Who could stand a whiff, let alone a draught of that sweet aroma?' somebody commented, increasing the volume of laughter in the council hall.

'Look, Fathers,' another man shouted, 'this is not the time for jokes. We're not paying this man with our milk for neglecting our cattle. Let's agree on one point – sack him and get a better one. As simple as that . . .'

The fact that Karekyezi had killed the lion was not considered by most as a matter of great importance. In their heated debate several of the villagers began talking at the same time. Then one man rose up to defend the kraalman.

'Fathers,' Tyagiri said, 'I've listened very carefully to all your arguments. It may be true that Karekyezi did not build his enclosure strongly enough to protect our cattle. It may be true, also, that he gets a bigger share of our milk which is, in fact, what he works for. But can't you see his brave deed – he saved us from that terrible enemy who was a great danger to our village? And has this man not served us faithfully for a long time . . .?'

'Yohoooo, faithfully . . .! Hear how he speaks,' a chorus drowned Tyagiri's words. 'Faithfully? By offering our cattle to wild beasts . . .?'

'Whatever you may plead for this jungleman, Tyagiri our friend,' Luyombo interrupted crossly, waving his arms in the air as if they were useless on his body, 'Karekyezi must go. We'll get another one to serve us faithfully.'

'Do you have any particular reason to say that?' Tyagiri asked the speaker.

'Yes, I have,' Luyombo replied. 'Why should your faithful man enrich himself at our expense? Suppose *we* had to look after those cattle by ourselves, milk the cows, sell the milk, don't you see how much money we would make daily? . . . And you're not even ashamed to call that man faithful?'

'Then why don't *you* take the job and do it for us and make yourself rich instead of employing another *mulaalo*?' Tyagiri retorted indignantly.

'An insult . . . an insult . . . sue him, Luyombo . . . sue him,' the council shouted angrily.

'Father,' Luyombo appealed to Mutwe-gwa-kyalo, 'Is this what you called us here for? For those who think themselves rich to insult us? Unless Tyagiri breaks his words I'll sue him right now before this council. How will people see me herding cattle? Me, a man with a full banana plantation, a coffee field, two wives and children, to herd Tyagiri's cattle! Does he imply that I'm out of my mind? Me, to do the job of an outcast . . .'

Before Mutwe-gwa-kyalo intervened Tyagiri countered calmly.

'Luyombo, Father, don't burst into flames like a fire. *You* suggested it yourself. I'm not in your mind to see or to know whether you're in or out of it . . .'

There was a fresh uproar. The whole council was thrown into confusion by Tyagiri's words. Everyone was shouting at the top of his voice.

'Tyagiri must break his words . . .'

'He's insulted us all through our friend . . .'

'Tyagiri must be fined a calabash of beer . . .'

'And a fat castrated goat . . .'

There was a little pause; this Tyagiri used as an opportunity to push forward his own plea.

'But, Father,' he said, turning to Mutwe-gwa-kyalo, 'if some of my friends feel that they've been insulted, I'll ask them to prove it. Then I'll apologize. But I have the right to say what I want. Luyombo also has the right to sue me. If the case goes against me I'll accept the fine . . .'

'But instead of going into a new issue,' the Chief said, 'Why don't you break what you've said to him, and let us proceed with our original discussion, the one that actually brought us here?'

'Father, that I can't do,' replied Tyagiri standing his ground.

'Why?' Mutwe-gwa-kyalo rebuked.

'Because I have a lot of witnesses, including you, Father, and Luyombo himself.'

'How do you mean?' The Chief asked sharply.

'Hasn't he openly spoken about herding the cattle, milking the cows, selling the milk and making much money daily? Were those not his own words? Haven't you all heard him?'

'Even if he said so,' an angry voice shouted from the rear, 'you've no right to push him into an outcast's job.'

'Then that's a matter of opinion,' Tyagiri responded. 'You can't stop a person doing what he wants, can you?'

Again a querrulous murmur arose in the hall, but no-one stood up to voice his complaints. This gave Tyagiri a chance to resume his plea for Karekyezi. Now he addressed the Chief.

'As I was saying, Father, Karekyezi is not lazy just because wild beasts break into his kraal or just because the cattle break out through it. In fact we owe this man our highest praises. When the whole village shook with his people's wild cries of alarm in the stillness of the night, which one of us went to help?'

Tyagiri's eyes swept the council hall to meet the challenge. Everybody looked back at him dryly, crossly, wrinkle-facedly.

'Therefore I suggest,' he continued, 'if it meets with your approval, we should give this man another chance. We are not certain that another *mulaalo* will be better. We can't just pick up a man about whom we know nothing. Suppose the new *mulaalo* steals our cattle and vanishes into the jungle among his kindred? Whose cattle have been marked? Don't they all look alike?'

There was a deep silence as his words began to sink into the minds of the gathering. Then he quickly made another suggestion which took the Chief by surprise.

'What I think the Chief should do is report the matter about this lion disaster to the Government. That is more important, don't you see my point?'

'Go on, let's hear it,' they roared.

'Well, they have guns and hunters. How do we know

34

there aren't more lions loitering about in the bush around this village? Suppose they come and attack?'

'Maybe. Maybe you're right, Father,' they agreed. 'The Government must be told immediately. This is very important. Our lives hang on that report.'

At this new turn of events Mutwe-gwa-kyalo dismissed the council. His motion had been defeated by one man who urged the council to send him, the Chief and landlord, on an errand he had not thought of.

'All right, all right,' the Chief said, 'if that's what you want. I'll ask the Gombolola Chief, sub-district officer, to send an army of Government hunters. The council is closed.'

It was after this meeting that word had reached Karekyezi. It was then that he had decided to retire, to leave the work of these half-hearted yeomen and masters.

'*Kaate rubura*,' he had sworn to his households, 'never trust these people however long you serve them. They'll always look for petty reasons to throw you out of your job. You all know the big hole Sepiriya is eating in our daily ration . . .'

They all knew the reason. One day before dawn a sturdy steer had broken through the kraal, leading a few other cattle out and into the village; they had browsed on Sepiriya's crop. Sepiriya had rounded up the animals, and had kept them in the heart of his banana plantation as hostages.

Karekyezi had frantically searched everywhere for the runaways, had scoured the whole area, until he traced them to Sepiriya's plantation.

'Even if you stand or dance on the point of a needle I'll not give the cattle back to you,' Sepiriya had told Karekyezi. 'This matter must be decided by the council, unless you pay me for the damage.'

Sepiriya had known that the herdsman had no money. The little which Karekyezi got from the sale of his

35

own milk he spent on his family's needs. Faced with Sepiriya's threat, Karekyezi had thought out a compromise. Since this mean person had no cattle of his own in any of the kraals around the village, Karekyezi would give him some milk and butter to prevent the matter reaching the village council.

'In that case,' Sepiriya had told the herdsman, 'you'll deliver *ekyanzi* of milk every day for a period of six months and *ensale* of butter every *diminika*, Sunday, for the same period . . .'

'Lord-of-mine,' Karekyezi said almost tearfully, 'you're a husband and a Father. You have a family to feed. You can afford that because you have this large banana plantation. Everywhere I look, those fat clusters of *matooke* make me feel hungrier. But have pity on your servant, Father. I've nowhere to get enough food to feed all those people I have at the kraal. Milk and butter is their only main food. If you take so much away they will starve, Father . . .'

'Look here, you man,' Sepiriya replied without batting an eyelid, 'what happens to your litter is none of my concern. Before you build weak enclosures for the cattle you should think of the consequences. Even now, by asking you to bring that little milk and butter, I'm doing you a favour. How on earth did you people grow up? Do you think I plant my crops to feed your masters' cattle?'

'Not that, Father,' Karekyezi went on pleading, 'Not that, lord-of-mine. I know it's my fault and I'm only pleading for those little stomachs I have to feed. They need their milk and . . .'

'I don't care whether your brats have little bellies or cooking-pot ones,' Sepiriya retorted, 'I don't even care if what they eat goes into their heads or legs. Don't waste my time. If you want the cattle back do what I've said or else the council will decide.'

36

'But Father,' Karekyezi fell on his knees, spreading out his arms as if to receive Sepiriya into them, 'How can I leave the cattle? I only wanted to tell you that the cows are not giving much milk these days because of the very little rain we have had . . .'

'Rain or no rain; grass or no grass,' Sepiriya exploded, 'what I've said is what I've said. And leave my homestead immediately if you don't accept my offer.'

Karekyezi remained silently on his knees; grains of tears stood in his eyes. Sepiriya's threat, mingled with the heat of the day, had suddenly wrung sweat from his body. He thought of the sudden starvation sweeping through his kraal. This man, Sepiriya, was thoughtless, depriving his family of their livelihood. The kraalman's eyes once more swept the drooping clusters of bananas and he sighed. This hardened farmer would not even give him one of the smallest clusters to take to his family to aid the vacuum that would be left by his demands. Slowly, the crestfallen Karekyezi stood on his feet, wiping the sweat with his hand and eyed the farmer.

Karekyezi had tried his best to plead with Sepiriya since the deal was too hard on his family. *Ekyanzi* of milk meant some two to three pints less for the family's daily needs. *Ensale* of butter meant more than five pounds knocked off the household's requirements.

Karekyezi, however, had no alternative but to agree. Kabahuma and the girls would have to beg for more solid foods, though these served merely as substitutes. A shortage of milk in the kraal was as bad as half-starvation.

It was these two incidents which had prompted him to check his cattle every morning to prevent further disasters.

FIVE

KAREKYEZI suddenly stopped dressing. He had already wound a clean calico around his waist and now he was putting the final touches to the second calico by knotting it over his left shoulder to cover his chest and back, leaving both arms bare. His two pieces of calico were clean in that, though they had not been washed since he bought them, he wore them only occasionally and Kabahuma always kept them neatly folded under the calf-skin on their bed.

Karekyezi had never worn shorts in his life. Shorts were unnecessary, expensive, useless, cumbersome when you had to spend the whole day roaming around in the pastures, feeding the cattle.

With his hand on the knot, Karekyezi turned to ask Kabahuma what she thought about his dress. Would he impress those village people at Lozio's beer party? But the words died on his lips, his hands relaxed on the knot, his eyes stared fixedly, as he watched her slowly undressing to expose her immense body to the freshness, the coolness, of the hut. The other members of the family were sitting outside under the shade of a thorn-tree in the *saazi*, eating the food she had brought back for them.

After Tereza's good hospitality and the little trip she had made to and from the village under that broiling sun, Kabahuma was now tired, sweating like a fat chicken roasting on a barbecue grill. By lying down completely naked on her bed she would be more comfortable and would have a good rest. But she had hardly lain down when Karekyezi peeled off his own clothes, and plunged his lank body in between her massive, sweating, slippery thighs. It was as if he had launched himself into the game of skating forwards and backwards.

He had taken her completely by surprise. But then, men were always awkward and employed awkward times to screw their women. Didn't men often pull their wives from the kitchen in order to have a quick one while the food was cooking? Didn't the so-called civilized men leave their guests in a drawing-room, enter the bathrooms where their wives were bathing, and screw them there, then return to carry on the conversation with their guests? Didn't they?

'But you're working on me too much these days, husband-of-mine,' Kabahuma complained sweetly, coaxingly, encouragingly; pretending not to welcome his attentions. 'Can't you see I'm tired from walking into the village? . . . Have you been chewing some herbs in the pastures? Have they sharpened your desire?'

'It's you, my bride. *You* have sharpened me. When you undress before me like that, do you expect me just to stand there and stare at this lovely body of yours without working on you, as if I was impotent?'

His hand was now working, his fingers gently pulling and stroking her natural strings. These she had elongated to some few inches by means of pulling at them with certain herbs when she reached puberty.

Her mother and aunties had taught her to do so, had told her it was one of the attractions men found on a woman's body, a sexual stimulant.

'Hihihihihi,' Kabahuma giggled invitingly, excitedly. 'Do they please you? You like them? Do they make your head drunk and your heart full of desire for me?'

'My desire grows so much that I feel flames of fire

39

eating my heart. Pushing the blood in my veins to all the parts of my body. Making my thing so stiff and hungry for yours . . .'

With that Karekyezi made a physical assault into the ready, accepting, yearning cave of her body. His wild, merciless thrusts mingled with their short quickened breaths and Kabahuma's own little cries of excitement and deep longing.

He tapped and thrust, tapped and thrust, tap, tap, tap . . . thrust . . . tap, tap, tap . . . thrust. She crooned. 'Ayiiii, my lord awuuuu, ayiiii. Harder, harder, ayiyiyiyi . . . ahhhh . . . ahhhh . . .' Tap, tap, tap . . . thrust . . . 'Ahhhh . . . ehuuu . . . ehuuu.'

Afterwards Karekyezi lay on his side for a little while, stroking the greasy, sweat-bathed mountain of flesh. Then, as if stung by a wasp, he sprang up, wiped his own sweat, then resumed dressing. Thirstily he gulped a few throatfuls of milk and felt better.

Kabahuma was quiet, flat on her back. She rolled her big, shining, beautiful eyes for a moment, then shut them. Apparently inviting sleep which would not be long in coming to her anyway.

Karekyezi was now fully dressed. With his stick in one hand, an empty gourd in the other, his inseparable clay-pipe in the mouth, he cast a quick glance at the calm figure stretched full length on the bed and smiled to himself. Quietly he went out of the hut and headed for the village, his tobacco pouch securely tucked in his loin calico.

Karekyezi never bought tobacco simply because he had enough of it growing around the hillock. He had thrown the seeds there on the day he arrived in the new settlement. It was Kabahuma's duty to pluck the ripe leaves occasionally, spread them under the sun to wither, trample on them on a dry goatskin, then spread them again to dry. She stored the tobacco wrapped up in an old piece of one of her spare blankets.

When Karekyezi or any member of his family smoked the tobacco you could smell its pungent aroma for some miles around. On calm mornings it hung heavily in the raw air for hours on end. No matter where or when he smoked it, it always seemed to milk Karekyezi's mouth dry for he would spit jet after jet of loose spittle unless he made a pause in his marathon smoking. Many a time he would complain of giddiness and of seeing the world rolling around him because of the strength contained in that tobacco.

'Kabahuma, what have you put in this tobacco,' he would ask her. 'My head is going round my body.'

'It's because you've not eaten anything, husband-of mine. Drink milk first . . .' Kabahuma would reply.

The people of Kayonga village connected anything dirty or foul with the cattle kraal. Non-smokers tended to complain that the older villager's tobacco smelled 'as horrid as a kraalman's'. Any part of the village which was not well looked after was described as 'as dirty as a kraal'. Faeces emptied by a drunken villager on the edge of the road were always blamed on the *mulaalo*.

When Karekyezi arrived at Lozio's party it was in full swing. Women had joined their husbands and were being looked after by the hostess Tereza. They were singing, talking loudly and cackling with laughter like mother hens.

Karekyezi squatted under the eaves of the house and eyed everybody thirstily; he waited impatiently. When he saw somebody drinking, he, too, would swallow a throatful of his own saliva. It was then that a man going by in a happy mood, a full gourd of *mwenge* in hand, called to the host.

41

'Lozio, come and get rid of this *mulaalo* squatting in front of your guests.'

Lozio came out of the house and saw Karekyezi.

'Hand me your gourd,' Lozio said. 'And don't squat in front of the people like that. When are you savages ever going to learn manners? . . . How are my cows? Eating a lot of grass?'

'Eeeeh, lord-of-mine,' Karekyezi responded meekly; he sat down properly, a forced smile spreading over his face, 'they're very fine, very healthy – good eaters of grass.'

His three-pint-sized gourd was filled up and handed back to him. The first few gulps sent two-thirds of the contents down his throat. Karekyezi smacked his lips, belched long and deep, and licked his mouth. After a short pause the gourd was back to his mouth, bottoms up, up, up . . . gulp, gulp, gulp. Then it was just dregs trickling on to his tongue; another long, sepulchral belch . . .

He looked into the gourd as if the drink was sticking inside there, saw the wet bottom and once more raised the container to his mouth. His host watched him in amazement.

'What! So quick! Do you think this is a beer well where you can drink like a frog?' he called out.

Karekyezi wiped his imaginary wet lips with his palm, cleared his throat, stroked it, and spoke.

'Lord-of-mine,' he said, 'it's the sun. It was roasting my throat. But you've saved me, Father.'

'But you must drink the way other people drink – slowly,' Lozio replied.

'Eeeeh, I've heard, father-of-twins . . .'

Karekyezi flattered his host who had never had the much cherished twins. It was a great honour to have twins born into the family and their birth was always celebrated with pomp in Kayonga village gathering people from the villages on the six neighbouring ridges.

42

As soon as the babies were born, a big *muyiro* – large amount – of *mwenge* was made. Goats and chickens were slaughtered in large numbers for the hundreds of guests who came. Many of these guests were uninvited and came from ridges lying four or five rivers away. They would know of the event only by word of mouth.

Drums thundered for the occasion and people converged on the homestead. It was like celebrating the home-coming of a long-lost relative who was offered a full bowl of water to drink on the threshold, and then told to plant a coffee bean by the side of the house to drive away the evil spirits which might have come with him.

At the twin-birth celebrations the rituals were different. The parents were given an everlasting title: for the father it was *Salongo* and for the mother it was *Nalongo*, added to their usual names to distinguish them from ordinary parents. The babies grew up with the only names given to twins. The first-born boy was *Wasswa* and the first-born girl was named *Babirye*. The next-born boy was called *Kato* and the next-born girl was *Nakato*.

During the celebrations *Salongo* and *Nalongo* danced with strands of bombo creeper around their necks and waists to drive away evil spirits. They sang aloud in obscene language as the men and women around them clapped madly to the rhythm of the throbbing drums.

SHE : *Salongo's big penis digs*
Deep into my womb;
Spits the seeds so hot,
Tickles and crushes the path.
My Salongo, Father, come,
Come and fuck me more

HE : *Nalongo's vagina is deep;*
My penis searches its corners,
Swims across to the end
Finds the place for my seeds.
Come, my Nalongo, come
Mother, I'll fuck you more

At such utterances drums and singers thundered to fortissimo, the singers, especially the women, adding as much obscenity as they could imagine. Then *Nalongo* would sit down with the babies on her lap, stretching out her legs to let *Salongo* hop twice across. He would then stand behind her and offer her *mwenge* from his own gourd, holding it with both hands to her mouth. At the end of the ritual all the kith and kin would jump into the arena and dance around the family.

Blessings were sung to the homestead and each spat in the air and at the twins to cleanse the homestead. If such blessings were not chanted and *Salongo* missed the ritual of hopping across his wife holding the babies, that was a bad omen. Either *abalongo* – babies would fly to the world of the beyond and never return – or their power would burn both the parents, leaving large ugly patches on their mouths, hands, feet and chests.

It was believed in Kayonga village, that whenever a person with these patches was seen, he or she had not properly completed the twin rituals. Observers would wag their tongues saying 'The twins burnt him . . . the twins burnt him.'

Many of the people of Kayonga were sure that Europeans had run away from their lands because they had been burnt by their twins and were ashamed of their colour. That was the reason why they called Europeans *emmomboze enjeru* – white vagabonds.

After successful completion of the twin ritual, food

was served and a last ritual performed. *Salongo* would dip a lump of *matooke* food into his own clay bowl of unsalted mushrooms and feed his wife and vice versa before anybody else ate their share. Food was followed by a drinking spree that went on until sundown. Before the guests left the homestead each one of them invoked God to take care of the babies and their parents.

From then on *Salongo* and *Nalongo* became respected parents. From time to time they were given presents because of the great boon they had conferred on the clan. In fact, every parent in Kayonga village wished for the day he would have twins in his family.

It was natural for Lozio to warm up at the name Karekyezi used and grinning at the flattery he took the empty gourd, and disappeared to replenish it. Karekyezi broadened his smile. In the process, and unmindful of a group of the villagers who sat a small distance away chatting, Karekyezi spat just out of a habit. One of the group saw him:

'Seen what that savage has done?'

'What has he done?' they asked, turning to see.

'Has spat.'

'What? Beer or spittle?'

'A thick lump of spittle.'

'Fool,' they shouted and hissed.

'These savage outcasts should never be allowed to come into the village,' one of them said.

'They live and behave like animals,' another one added.

'Even our elders never shared food or drinks with them,' a third man said, rising up, 'I'll show him manners.' The man walked up to Karekyezi, slapped him across the face, and asked, 'Does it smell, what you drink, eh? . . . Why don't you go to drink the cow's urine?'

The whole episode took place so quickly that

45

Karekyezi did not know what to answer. Clearly, he had not meant to offend anybody. Moreover, he was in their village, had come to beg for their *mwenge*, it was better to keep silent.

Just then Lozio came back to find the other man hovering over the poor kraalman, talking in high words.

'Lozio,' the man spoke angrily, 'turn away this man.'

'What has he done?' asked Lozio.

'Has spat a big lump of spittle in front of us as if we smelt like him and his kraal.'

'But, lord-of . . .' Karekyezi tried to defend himself, but his words were cut short by Lozio's guest.

'If you want your man to stay, we shall go.'

Lozio, however, was one of the villagers who had entrusted Karekyezi with his cattle. He could not simply get rid of the man who was looking after 'the other side of the house'. On the other hand Lozio could not afford to see his village companions deserting him simply because the kraalman had squirted a lump of spittle, which was a habit of these people as anybody in the village knew. Thinking fast, however, he reached a quick decision.

'Karekyezi, take this beer and go and sit behind the kitchen. And you, Fathers, you know the habits of these people, forget him. Let's drink our *mwenge*; I still have plenty in the house. We'll drink until we bring down the sun and until we bring it up again.'

That settled the matter immediately. But because the day was hot, and drinking on an empty stomach, Karekyezi was soon drunk. He started talking bravely to everybody, promising each one *ekyanzi* of milk or *ensale* of butter. A trick that got him more beer from their gourds. He returned to the house, and went down on both knees at the door.

'Father-of-twins,' he addressed his host, 'let the Giver-of-life give you more children. Live long; let your

46

body grow old, but not your hand that gives. I'll take the most care of your cattle. Your cows will double their calves . . .'

He started singing sweet nothings to entertain Lozio and his guests; he jumped up and down like an Australian kangaroo. Then he moved away, and sat down against a banana tree. Lozio's children were playing nearby with a host of other village children. They began teasing him. They screamed uproariously when he imitated a monkey's antics, scratching his face, his armpits and his backside. Suddenly the children shouted, prompting the adults to turn and look and see what they had seen.

'Sit well, you fool,' they roared at him.

'Oh, oh, oh,' the women screamed, 'the man has killed us. He's shown us his hanging things, oh!'

At that instant a man rushed forward with a stick. Karekyezi sprang up drunkenly and in the process his loin calico loosened, leaving him stark naked. There was a wild uproar, the women scattering themselves in all directions to hide their faces behind the banana trees. The man who had threatened to beat him up, burst out laughing raucously. The others laughed too. Karekyezi, joining in the laughter, gathered his calico unconcernedly, and rewound it around himself ceremoniously. Then, as if nothing had happened, he returned to his drink and sang to himself. A few minutes later he entered the kitchen, lit his pipe, and reappeared smoking peacefully.

'To hell!' all the people shouted when the smell of the tobacco reached their nostrils. 'Take that horrid tobacco to the bush, you foolish idiot . . .'

Their yelling brought out Lozio who had no alternative but to dismiss Karekyezi from his home, to appease his guests.

'But, lord-of-mine,' Karekyezi begged, 'at least give me another drop, father-of-twins. Will you simply push away your servant with an empty gourd? Shall I not take some to your bride Kabahuma . . .? You're my master . . . you give me everything. What do others give me? Insults and slaps and beatings . . .'

At last Lozio replenished the gourd.

'If you drink so stupidly I'll never again give you my beer,' he said.

But Karekyezi in his drunken mood was not impressed. He simply went away whistling, singing merrily and jumping . . . springing like an antelope. He went straight back to his kraal, where he exchanged a few sweet words with Kabahuma, and sang and danced for her. Minutes later he was snoring like a group of hungry roaring lions.

SIX

As the sun began to descend towards its abyss the small, sparsely-scattered white fields of clouds began to gather together. They formed themselves into a massive, dark, rolling mountain and rumbled as if an infinite hand was folding the dried skin of a colossal mammoth. Roaring like a huge team of hungry lions the dark mountain soon swallowed up the bright sunrays and within minutes it had opened all its pores to release a blinding downpour.

The cattle, which had hitherto been mooing to each other as they munched the grass, suddenly stopped; their movements paralysed by the torrent. Inch by inch they got together. Body against body, seeking each other's warmth. Then they stood still, providing their keepers with the much-sought-after shelter. The rain poured and poured and poured.

'This is what they don't understand in the village,' loud-mouthed Kagabu told his older companions as they all clustered under the legs of the cattle. 'The sun roasts our bodies. Snakes look for our blood. Now the rain folds us under the cattle as if we were chicks under their mothers' wings.'

'But we can't stay here all the time,' replied Barigye, always the boss whenever Karekyezi left them with the cattle in the pastures. 'We are used to this. We have to move on as soon as this torrent passes. You know this kind

49

of downpour doesn't last. Let's stand in it and wash our bodies, then we won't feel it.'

So saying, Barigye tore off his drenched loin calico and stood perfectly naked under the rain. He rubbed every part of his body with his hands and now and then he turned his head skywards, trapping the rain-water in his mouth which he formed into a funnel.

His young companions were fascinated. Excitedly, each one threw off his calico and followed suit. They giggled and grinned happily; they jumped up and down, extending their arms upwards as if to bring every drop of the rain down on to their bodies. Then they amused themselves with jokes thrown at Barigye.

'Aweee, Barigye. But you've got such a long one.'

'It's like that of a bull!'

'I wonder how his bride will enjoy it when he marries.'

'She will cry "awuuuu, Barigye you kill me . . ."'

'And if it's not as strong and long like that of a bull,' Barigye replied before the rest joined in, 'who will give me his daughter to marry? Don't brides love to cry sweetly and dance on it when it's so stiff and hungry?'

They all roared with laughter which was suddenly clapped back into their mouths by a thunderbolt. They scampered back to the safety of the shelter provided by the cattle, each winding his calico around his loins. They squatted on their haunches, doubled into human balls, waiting. They were steaming heavily and shaking; their teeth chattering. Then, just as suddenly as it had come, the rain began to cease. The massive dark mountain overhead rolled away slowly, farther and farther, rumbling, roaring, thundering.

The young herdsmen then drove the cattle from the pastures to the marsh where they watered them for hours. They passed the time by whistling to them and singing to them sweetly. Barigye as a soloist sang the names of each bull, connecting each one with a cow, his companions entreating the cattle in a chorus.

Solo.   *My cow Bishaza has filled her belly;*
The fine grass makes her skin shine.
Her lover is my handsome bull Rugaju,
He loves his beautiful bride Bishaza.

Chorus: *Drink, my handsome bulls.*
Drink, my beautiful cows.
I'll not drink before you do;
This water was made for you.

As if in response to the song each animal named lowed over and over again. They drank to their hearts' content as the herdsmen went on singing the chorus, whilst giving each animal its share of water from a halved gourd.

The ground was boggy and slippery, and the herdsmen fell many times while trying to scoop the water from the pond. They swore and spat. But it was the sort of thing they were used to every day of their lives. They had to bear the extreme heat of the day; they had to brave torrential downpours; all for the small share of the milk that was their main food.

Later on they drove the cattle back to the kraal. The cattle knew exactly what to do before entering the enclosure – stay in the *saazi* until all the cows were milked. When milking was over each member of the family drank the unboiled milk to his satisfaction and Kabahuma sent the boys into the village to fetch the food Tereza had promised to give to the family.

In the meantime Kabahuma took all the milk that remained and emptied it into a large churning-calabash. She was quite an expert in producing sour milk and butter and had learnt the skill under her mother's tuition when

51

she was a little girl. Now she was passing the knowledge on to the younger girls in her kraal.

The girls watched her at work, tossing the big calabash forth-and-back, forth-and-back, forth-and-back. The flesh of her fat upper arms dancing loosely with each movement. Back-and-forth, back-and-forth, back-and-forth, the bottom of the calabash went on singing.

As the milk began to coagulate, Kabahuma changed it into a wide-mouthed calabash and churned again. Then she paused for some time to allow it to settle. She then scooped the curds with her hand, separating them from the whey, and put the curds into each *ensale*. In a day or two the butter would be ready for use and sale. She offered the whey to the children to drink; it went well with the roasted cassava and sweet-potatoes which the older boys had prepared under the hot ashes. By then the pot was steaming on the three hobs chipped from a near-by ant-hill.

Karekyezi's clanswomen always used old butter to smear their bodies with, making them soft, smooth, tender and attractive to their menfolk. Who wanted to marry a woman with a rough, manly skin? Men were smeared with butter only when they were young children – to help them sleep soundly, their skins and muscles relaxed.

At last the boiling food in the pot was ready – cassava, sweet-potatoes and beans. Kabahuma cut two orange-sized lumps of butter and dropped them into the pot, then with her wooden ladle she distributed the food to everyone in clay bowls. They ate, drinking milk in between, the children sniffing and wiping their running noses with their small hands.

Karekyezi was still deep in his slumberland when the eating activities took place. At times he would roar like the engine of an ancient automobile suddenly revved into life and the children would burst out giggling.

'Sssshhh,' Kabahuma would warn them. 'Don't

laugh so loud. Let him rest. You know he wakes up before the day opens its eyes . . .'

When everybody had had his fill, the children began to yawn and drowse, but when Kabahuma sent them to bed they protested.

'It's a long time since *Tata* slept,' they said. 'Won't he tell us some stories tonight?'

'Haven't you got ears?' Kabahuma rebuked them. 'I'll tell you a story instead . . .'

Kabahuma was as expert in spinning folklore as she was in churning butter. She had inherited a rich store of tell-tales from her parents, her grandparents, and even from Karekyezi's mother long before the old woman died. Anyone could start a tale and she would correct them immediately they went wrong, then she would take it up to the end. Her way of bumping into other people's story-telling often annoyed Karekyezi. Whenever she did so, he would growl and say; 'Our wise woman of the kraal kingdom!'

But the children enjoyed the way she snatched a tale from her husband. So they would ask him to 'Bring a story, *Tata*,' then tip Kabahuma the wink when part of the story was to be sung, for she thrilled them with her singing, which was as beautiful as a nightingale's.

This evening everybody gathered near the hearth to hear her new story.

'Once upon a time,' she began, 'there lived a king called Mugabe. He was rich, powerful and kind. He named his country after his own name.

'King Mugabe had a lot of cattle, women and children. His cattle were as many as the sand of the earth, his women as many as the stalks of grass, and his children as many as the stars in the sky.

'His people loved him because he gave them plenty of meat. But those who did not come on time when the cows were slaughtered went away with hoofs, while his hunters and warriors gathered all the tendons for their bow-strings.

'King Mugabe gave the skins to young people for their dresses. Some of them rubbed their skins with butter to make them soft, but those who did not have enough butter left the skins as they were given to them. When they walked their skins sang on their backs, *ndibati, ndibati, ndibati,* because they were hard and dry.

'The king loved to hear the song of their skins, so he made these young men the herdsmen of his cattle. He told them to march before him every day before they took his cattle into the pastures.

'Then, suddenly, the rains began to disappear and there was not enough water in his land although the cows were still giving plenty of milk. So the king told his wives to bathe his children with the milk of the cows. When the children were thirsty and wanted water their mothers begged the cows to make more urine for them to drink.

'During that time food became scarce, so the king's wives made so much butter that it covered the whole world like the highest mountains of the earth. The king allowed everybody in his kingdom to eat from these mountains of butter.

'As children grew up in his land, they became the most beautiful girls and most handsome boys – they were fat and healthy because of the milk and butter. But because there was no more rain coming, King Mugabe became sad.

'Then some of his cattle began to die. He called all the people in Mugabe Kingdom and ordered them to weep and wail. After seven days of weeping and wailing, King Mugabe gave each family a number of cattle.

' " May you have more cattle to cover the earth," the king said. "Go and find better pastures and let your children and grandchildren protect their cattle against all kinds of danger. Teach them to love their cattle first, then their new families, because those families will grow on the milk and butter given by their cows."'

'Then the people of Mugabe began to move into other lands looking for new pastures. As they searched for them they sang, begging all the birds and the winds to tell them where they could graze their cattle.

> *'Tell us little birds,*
> *Tell our cows and bulls;*
> *Tell us oh gentle winds,*
> *Where have you seen green pastures?*
> *Where have you seen fine grass?*
>
> *There, oh good herdsmen;*
> *There, oh cows and bulls,*
> *Over the highland hills,*
> *The hills of Kooki land,*
> *The hills of Kabula land,*
> *Mawogola is another land.*
>
> *What have you seen?*
> *Tell us gentle winds;*
> *Lead us little birds,*
> *To those yonder lands,*
>
> *Come, oh good herdsmen,*
> *You'll feed the cows and bulls,*
> *Where the rain is plenty*
> *Over the highland plains,*
> *Where the rivers are bursting.*

'So the people of Mugabe found the new lands, and roamed in them feeding their cattle. But they had no food of their own and they had to beg for it. The people in these lands were rich and lived in beautiful villages and in exchange for food they began to take all the cattle of the new people, but refused to let them live in their villages.

'However, Mugabe's people knew how to look after cattle and the people in the villages appointed them as keepers of the cattle they had taken; they told them to build their homes and live in the bush. And so, the new people became the servants and keepers of other people's cattle.'

The children had listened in awe. Then they asked Kabahuma:

'Where are those people now, Mama? Can't they run away with their cattle?'

'You'll know who those people are when you grow up, my children. You'll know what they do to get back their cattle. Now it's time for you to go to bed.'

Of course, the bigger boys and girls knew who those people were. They remembered what Karekyezi had often told them about building themselves new stocks of cattle if they were to shake off their poverty.

Karekyezi himself had done so and was still passing stolen, newly-born calves to the kraals of his relatives living with large herds far away in the hills. Herds of their own, now regained.

SEVEN

ONE evening not long after his visit to Lozio's, Karekyezi went to Tyagiri's house to give him news of his cattle.

'Lord-of-mine,' he said, 'I think that two of your cows will soon give birth and I've come for some salt for them. Will you come to the kraal to see them?'

'Do you think they're going to give birth tonight?' asked Tyagiri.

'Not really tonight. But I only wanted to bring the information to you as I always do,' replied Karekyezi.

Tyagiri had known that two of his cows were pregnant. Karekyezi had told him and he had gone to the kraal to see them a few weeks before. Now he was happy that the time had at last come. The number of his cattle was growing in the care of this faithful *mulaalo*.

'Thank you, Karekyezi, thank you for the news,' he said. 'I'll come tomorrow morning before the cattle leave the *saazi*. Now take the salt . . .'

He gave Karekyezi the salt he needed for the cows. This salt always served a double purpose; not all of it was given to the animals; some was used by the family in their food in order to eke out the salt which Karekyezi had bought with his own little money from the sale of milk.

'When one of my cows gives birth to two calves,' Tyagiri told Karekyezi, 'I'll give you one, provided it's a bull. You've served us well and I'll bring this idea to the council. You can always sell the bull and get some money...'

57

'Ayiyiyiyi, lord-of-mine,' said Karekyezi jumping for joy, 'what can I say about your kind heart! I love cattle. I have always wanted to have some. How could I sell my lord's gift?'

'But if the council agrees with my idea, Karekyezi, how many bulls will you keep if you don't sell them?' asked Tyagiri.

'Maybe some of my lords will give me a baby cow in one season or another. Then my bulls will be active and get me some calves . . .'

'Oh, no, Karekyezi. Don't believe that. Nobody in this village will ever give you a baby cow. You know that. The only thing that you can do, perhaps, is to exchange your bulls for cows among your friends. Nobody will agree to exchange bulls for cows in this village, I tell you . . .'

Karekyezi went back to his kraal and told Kabahuma all that had taken place in the village. She was pleased with the news.

'Oh, husband-of-mine,' she said happily, 'some of these people are really good and kind to us . . .'

'Yes,' Karekyezi's words bumped into hers, 'but they're stupid. Suppose these two cows calve tonight, you think I would rush into the village to tell him? Just because he's going to give me a bull? Have I not got enough bulls already?'

Tyagiri, however, was as good as his word. He arrived the next morning and inspected the two cows with keen interest. Yes, their bellies were really big and the cows healthy and strong. He grinned and nodded his head approvingly. He wondered who would be able to predict the cows' exact time of giving birth? Could this expert herdsman do it? Could he tell the time, judging from his long experience? Tyagiri smiled as the herdsman watched him amusedly, then asked with hopeful enthusiasm:

'When do you think the calves will come Karekyezi?

And can you tell how many, judging by the cows' big bellies?'

'Well, I should say in about two to three days we should see the calves,' said Karekyezi putting a punch into his employer's hopes. 'But I can't say how many are likely to come, Father.'

'Why not?' Tyagiri asked surprised. 'You can't say? From all that experience you have?'

'Father, I'll tell you something. The size of the bellies of pregnant cows does not always tell the truth. Cows are like our women. They get big bellies and then what? One child. Others get small bellies and give birth to twins, you see?' explained Karekyezi.

'Hahahaha,' Tyagiri laughed heartily, nodding his head, 'I think you're right there, Karekyezi. When I put twins into the belly of my youngest wife, was that belly not small? Hahahaha.'

Karekyezi laughed too, as if he had witnessed the incident. He was happy that his words had carried weight and that his employer had agreed with him.

'Then let me know as soon as possible before they give birth.' Tyagiri said, 'I want to be present. By the way, can they still go to the pastures? Don't they make you walk behind them like a snail?'

'That's not a problem for a cow,' Karekyezi explained. 'She follows the others, then her time arrives and suddenly she slackens her walk; she lies down and, pronto, the baby is coming . . .'

As Karekyezi spoke he demonstrated each movement. How the cow followed the others to the pastures; how she slackened her steps; how she lay down to deliver her offspring. He demonstrated as if he himself was the cow in action. Then, as if to drive a convincing point home, he said to Tyagiri:

'But these two still look strong. There's plenty of time

for them if I'm not mistaken; at best we should see their beautiful ones within two days. I'll come for you before our new little guests arrive.'

In the late morning hours of that same day one of the cows began to show the signs. Karekyezi had been keeping a watchful eye on both cows, and now he told the boys to round them up and keep a close watch on them. Soon afterwards the cow gave birth to two young ones, a baby bull and a baby cow. Karekyezi and his group nursed the animals carefully, tenderly. They remained with them until late in the afternoon.

'Barigye,' he called to his sinewy, strong brother, 'take this calf to Rweza's kraal immediately. You other lads go and water the cattle. Kagabu, come with me, we have to return the mother and the other calf to the kraal . . .'

Tenderly, Karekyezi carried the calf in his arms. Its mother followed him and Kagabu brought up the rear. They made twists and turns through the pastures until they came to the kraal. Kabahuma was just outside, watching her children playing, her arms akimbo.

'I told you, you see?' Karekyezi spoke to her gleefully. 'Did we not say this one would not go through the day? And what a beautiful little cow she has given to us! I've already sent the baby to Rweza's kraal and I'm going into the village to tell Tyagiri . . .'

'How about the other cow?' Kabahuma asked, a broad smile lighting her entire face. 'Is she not yet ripe?'

'That one should calve during the night, I think,' replied Karekyezi. 'We'll see. We must watch out.'

'But he said he would be present to see his cows giving birth?' she reminded questioningly.

'Who, Tyagiri? As if you didn't know them! Would he be the first to come here at night? Have I not told you many times that they cannot use their heads, woman?'

'But I'm only repeating what he said . . .'

'Forget about what he said,' broke in Karekyezi. 'First they say a kraal smells like their shit; but they like its milk and butter. Secondly, they're scared to leave the village at night even if their hearts think of their cattle. Thirdly, I told him to expect his calves in two days. You think this is the first time any of them is going to use his head?'

'But with the news of this one, he will surely expect that the other cow is also ready?' persisted Kabahuma.

'What's the matter with you, woman?' asked Karekyezi. 'Are you like *them*? Can't you use your head properly? If two women are pregnant at the same time, must they give birth at the same time or on the very same day . . .?'

'No, but you planted some hope into his heart,' Kabahuma went on.

'And what if I did? Am I a miracle worker, or am I inside the stomachs of the cows, to know exactly what time their calves must come? Women! Can't you forget him and rejoice? Is our stock not growing larger and larger?' Karekyezi was dying with excitement. 'Do you know how many we have now? Plenty! If we gather them all from the five kraals of our people, we should have ... let me count ...'

There was a pause as he counted his booty on his fingers, ticking away with a nod of his head how many were in which kraal. Then he spoke loudly:

'Yes, ninety-one, with the *one* that has come today. Maybe I should count ninety-two . . .'

'Don't raise your spear before you see the enemy,' Kabahuma warned with a well-known proverb.

'And how many has Tyagiri got here?' he asked in ridicule and immediately answered his own question. 'Not half of what we have! Hihihihi, *kaate rubura, nyabura.*'

Tyagiri was not at home late that afternoon, so Karekyezi passed the message to his chief wife.

'My bride,' he said as humbly as he could, 'I'm very happy but a little surprised. Surprised because I didn't expect it to happen so soon, very happy because one of my master's cows has given birth this very *afternoon.*'

He stopped abruptly, and watched her reaction. Her face was all smiles. She stopped her task of preparing the evening meal, and fell into conversation with Karekyezi.

'Congratulations, Karekyezi. What calves?'

'What calf, my bride, not two or three. Just one calf. A bull.'

'Oh,' Tyagiri's wife exclaimed and then added quickly, 'But why are you so happy? My husband told me he was to give you a baby bull if his cows had more than one calf each. I don't think he'll give you that *one*?'

'Oh, no, no, no, my bride, that's not what makes me happy. It's because my great anxiety about pregnant cows has now been partly allayed. Sometimes cows, like human females, get complications. They may die or their calves may die during the birth. But this one did it perfectly normally. And what a fine baby bull!'

'But my husband told me that their bellies were so big that he expected each cow would deliver two or even three calves!' exclaimed Tyagiri's wife.

At this Karekyezi burst out laughing until tears began to roll down his face. He shook his head, coughing and choking, slapped the pain in his ribs and then spoke:

'My bride, do you want to kill me with laughter?' he said.

'What is there to laugh at?' she replied.

'My bride, that was a preposterous anticipation by my master. Is a cow not like a woman? Do not some women grow large stomachs when they're pregnant? But how many or how often have they produced twins or triplets?'

His statement provoked her shrill laughter which he

62

joined with his raucous one, throwing back his head, wiping away his tears and roaring again.

'All right, all right,' she said when their joint laughter died down, 'I'll tell your master. But wait, I think I have a drop of beer in the house. Let me congratulate you with it . . . by the way, how about the other cow? When is she going to show us the fruit of her bowels?'

'That, my bride, I can't say exactly. The one today surprised me so much that I've no words left in my mouth. Maybe in a day or two . . .' lied Karekyezi.

He took his drink almost in one gulp, thanked her profusely, and hurried back to the marsh where his juniors were watering the herd. He inspected the other cow, but it seemed that its time had not come yet. She drank as usual and walked safely back to the kraal.

As Karekyezi had expected, Tyagiri came back that evening to see his new calf. He cracked some jokes with both Kabahuma and Karekyezi. He again thanked Karekyezi for delivering his cow safely, and cracked the last joke.

'When a cow gives birth inside this kraal,' he said, 'I think this place turns into a kind of maternity hospital. You two work like a busy doctor and midwife. And all the boys and the girls play nurses. You see what I mean? . . . I would like to watch you all working on my cow, so don't take her into the pastures until her time comes . . . and I have a feeling she will give us more than one.'

Both man and wife exchanged a quick glance, and each killed an eye when Tyagiri was not looking, then they smiled. They were not worried, of course. It was clear he had not suspected foul play with the first cow. Since no telepathy existed between him and the cattle how would he know that the herdsman had deprived her of her sweet little baby? How would he know they had robbed him? Was that not the right course for the kraalmen to steer into

63

their future? Were they not retrieving their long-lost property?

When Tyagiri left them, both man and wife started making preparations. Their long experience with cattle had taught them how to detect the symptoms of a pregnant cow, and they would isolate her to a better place when her time to deliver arrived. Kabahuma was always ready with some herbs she had plucked in readiness for delivering the pregnant cow and these were brewed in a halved gourd with some salt in the mixture.

Tyagiri had unconsciously hinted at her midwifery skill, and Kabahuma knew every bit of it. She was always the first to clear the nostrils of a newly-born calf, blowing into them with her own breath; this she did every time a new calf was born in her presence. She would then let the mother cow lick her young one all over, washing it with the tongue. While this went on, Kabahuma would attend to the cow itself – washing it with the prepared herbs and gently pushing back that bloody part of the womb hanging outside.

After this Kabahuma cleaned the cow's teats with some more herbs, then fed the cow other brewed herbs mixed with *ekisula*, a crude salt. This, Kabahuma said, helped the cow to have more milk in the udder. After the newly-born calf had suckled, Kabahuma would separate it from its mother and keep it in her own hut, not far from the fireplace. Here the calf enjoyed the warmth of the fire and slept soundly and peacefully like a human baby. Later, when the calf was strong enough and bouncing about healthily, Kabahuma would transfer it to the smaller hut built for calves opposite the family hut.

Every morning and evening Kabahuma released all the calves into the *saazi* after her husband and the boys had milked the cows to allow them to suckle. She did this until the calves were old enough to follow their mothers into the pastures where their first experience was to get acquainted with the mongrel dogs. These dogs perpetually followed and pestered the calves because of their dung which gave off the smell of the milk they suckled rather than of the soft grass they nibbled.

Karekyezi had two such underfed dogs. They always crouched, and folded themselves like living balls, in the warm ashes by the fireside. He had kept them without any proper care, untrained and useless. Karekyezi's dogs would even run for refuge at the slightest hooting of an owl, and a distant laughing hyena always made them whine like whipped children.

Karekyezi had kept these two dogs simply because he had picked them up as babies from the scrub where somebody, apparently, had dumped them. Karekyezi had seen the cattle lowering their noses to the ground around a flame tree without eating the grass. Then he had heard the whining and had come and rescued the two little creatures.

When he took them, he had thought that the whimpering things would grow into useful dogs; that they would automatically turn into protectors of the kraal. They would be ferocious, would bark and bite and fight wild animals. But both Kabahuma and her husband were disappointed when the puppies grew up. In spite of the family's share of milk Kabahuma fed them on, the two little dogs never showed any sign of ferocity. She had, therefore, seen no reason why she should go on feeding the mongrels. Even so, there they stayed, if they did not go into the village to look for bones. Once in the village they mixed with the village dogs and the pack followed the cattle in the pastures, feasting and fighting over the calves' dung.

Just towards midnight, Tyagiri's second cow gave birth to two baby bulls. Since Karekyezi and Kabahuma knew that they would get one of the calves, there was no point in rushing it away to a kinsman's kraal. Moreover, Karekyezi wanted to play his part of the faithful *mulaalo* as well as he could so that same night he went into the village to report to Tyagiri who was already in bed.

'This really beats me, my lord,' Karekyezi reported impressively, 'I just woke up to check the cattle and there was my lord's cow in labour. There was not even time to come for you as everybody was busy running here and there, Father. You'll excuse me for that?'

'All right, all right . . . and did you say they're both bulls?' Tyagiri asked with a yawn.

'Eeeeh, Father. I'm afraid the season hasn't been very good for my lord . . .'

'Never mind, Karekyezi. Bulls are also cattle. I'll come in the morning to see them and then give you one of them as I promised . . .'

'Ayiyiyi . . . ayiyiyi, my lord, I'm so happy, so happy, Father,' Karekyezi went down on his knees. 'Thank you for always, Father. I'll never forget you in my life. I'll keep my lord's beautiful gift. I'll tell all my people about your kind heart. Ayiyiyi . . . ayiyiyi. Let the Giver-of-life keep his hand over your roof, yourself and your offspring. Ayiyiyiyiyi . . .'

EIGHT

KAREKYEZI's long life with cattle had created a kind of telepathy between them. He often talked with them and he understood them and they understood him. Sometimes they clashed with him, but he always explained the situation and tried to convince them that what he did was right.

They knew he would leave them some day; he had told them so. He had taken good care of them for a long time. He had saved them from all kinds of danger but now he had grown old and his masters would not care for his old age, nor for his future.

As he inspected and fondled them early one morning, Karekyezi had a long discussion with the herd before letting them out of the kraal to go to the *saazi*. Steers and heifers sympathized with him, but the old bulls and cows clashed with him. They accused him of stealing their babies during all those years they had known him.

'But can't you understand me?' he reasoned with them, 'I did not mean to hurt you, fathers and mothers. Haven't you all been good to me and to my family? But how would you expect me to live without fathers and mothers like you to look after me in my old age? Since I couldn't take you with me, wasn't it wise for me to take the young ones to be my future fathers and mothers . . .?'

All the cattle lowed; of course they understood the reason. They often met their stolen young ones in the pastures but the little ones never knew who gave them their blood and flesh. They had become strangers to their parents. Why didn't Karekyezi explain first before he stole the calves?

Karekyezi replied, although his heart was breaking with shame. He told them that they should see his point and sympathize with him. He would certainly take the greatest care of their offspring in the years to come, and treat them in the same way he had treated their parents. He would never allow anybody with bad intentions to touch them.

Karekyezi reminded the cattle of the fate that awaited the cows who no longer gave milk; the bulls who no longer mounted their beloved ones to produce calves. Would they not be called too old? Would they not be slaughtered in the village as had happened only a few days ago? Had not the village people come to the kraal and led away an old bull?

The cattle lowed questioningly. They had seen their brother being led away. He had never returned. Now they wanted to know exactly what had happened to him so Karekyezi supplied the answer. The people in the village had killed him and had feasted on his meat. They had jumped for joy, danced, sung and drunk, then they had passed his bones to their dogs . . .

'Mooooooooo,' the cattle moaned.

Then Karekyezi tried even harder to win their sympathy. Had he not given his life in order to protect the herd against wild beasts and snakes . . .? 'Moooooo . . .'

When he and his brothers killed the terrible lion, did his masters come to help in the battle . . .? 'Nooooo . . .,

Karekyezi next turned against his employers. Did they not care only for their wives, children and domestic animals which lived with them in the village . . .?

'Moooo . . . moooo . . .'

Did they not give special treatment to their hunting

68

dogs, goats and chickens by allowing them to live with them in their very houses? And did these give those people milk and butter?

'Nooooo . . .' every time Karekyezi asked a question the cattle moo'd their agreement or disagreement.

When leopards attacked and killed dogs and goats in the village, did not the village people shout their heads off and hunt and kill the beasts . . .? When kites and hawks threatened the chickens, did not the whole village raise hell to drive away those birds of prey . . .?

The cattle still remembered the lion incident. The beast had forced his way into the kraal and had strangled their fat sister, dragging her carcass out. Karekyezi and his households had been fast asleep at the time and now, in perfect unison, the cattle conveyed to him what had actually happened that night.

They had smelled the lion and had tried to call for Karekyezi's help. They were terrified. They had stampeded all over the place, lowing fearfully. It was then that all the calves had broken loose, and had invaded his hut, pleading for help in their terrified young voices. It was during this fracas that the whole household had woken up.

Then Karekyezi took over the story, conveying the rest of it to the cattle. When they had woken up every man had grabbed a couple of spears and sticks and, as nude as he had slept, had made his way through the excited calves and out of the hut. All the cattle had been in a state of a frenzy.

Then, with the help of the moonlight, slowly, carefully and quietly they had searched for the intruder. It was then that Karekyezi had espied a gaping hole in the enclosure and had stealthily gone near, and listened . . .

The beast had been there, as sure as a tongue in his mouth. It was enjoying a meal, crushing the bones of his stolen meat. Karekyezi had beckoned to his companions and one by one, carefully and slowly, they had crawled through the hole, each taking his position to prepare for the battle.

Then they had seen the lion devouring his meat unsuspectingly, busily, hungrily, greedily. He was swallowing big chunks . . .

At this sad information the cattle lowed their lamentation, 'Mooooooooo.'

Then Karekyezi told the animals how he had declared the war. He had gone out to the beast, whistling for his companions to get ready, and then he had thrown a stick straight at the lion. Everything from then on had happened so suddenly, so quickly, so fast . . .

The beast had raised his head and had seen the intruder. Whoever it was, the beast had seemed to say, whoever wanted to disturb others at meal times, had better be given a sound lesson. This was no ordinary meal; when the king of the jungle feasted all he wanted was peace.

The next moment had seen the lion reacting furiously. His muzzle and his big, powerful paws had all been bathed in blood. His tail had wagged in uncontrollable rage. He had swallowed the big succulent steak he was eating, licked the warm tasty blood on his muzzle, had growled fearfully and had sprung for Karekyezi.

The beast was now airborne; its sharp claws dripping with the cow's blood. The claws were spitting out tongues of vengeance, sticking out of their paws like poisoned arrows. They were ready to turn Karekyezi into a mass of flesh and bones, a pulp, a meat salad, a lion's dessert. With incredible agility and expertise, Karekyezi had let go of one of his three-feet long, razor-sharp spears. Simultaneously, he had shouted one short alarm, a signal to his companions. At the same time he had side-stepped to get out of the way of the huge bestial landing craft.

Karekyezi had known and had expected what had

followed his challenge. His heart had turned into steel, his sinewy arms had gathered all the power he had in every nook of his body. Either he or the lion had to die.

The lion had hardly touched down when a thunder of alarms rent the stillness of the night. Karekyezi's companions had sprung up from their positions shouting. They had thrust all their razor-sharp spears hard into the beast but Karekyezi's first spear had found its intended home. It was firmly fixed through the lion's heart.

The womenfolk had rushed to the scene with flaming torches of dried reeds and grass uttering wild alarms . . . agitated, ear-splitting ululations. They had hugged their menfolk, and had rubbed their backs and arms with butter. The enemy was no more.

Karekyezi paused, stopped suddenly, and the cattle lowed more lamentations. Now they knew how much he loved them.

'Mooooo . . . moooooo . . . mooooo,' they approved.

NINE

TOWARDS the end of a routine meeting of the village council Tyagiri suddenly raised an unexpected point.

'Fathers,' he said, 'I know that what I'm going to say may have nothing to do with what we've been discussing. But I'm only asking you to give it your serious consideration. In my view I think it's important.'

Everybody pricked up their ears, their eyes were glued on him. This man again, with his abrupt ideas, Mutwe-gwa-kyalo thought. He always wants to influence this council against me. How many times have I had to run like a whipped small boy, carrying his wishes to the Government? Him again!

'Fathers,' Tyagiri proceeded, 'from today's meeting we've learnt that we're soon to cast off poverty from the back of our village. Our many bananas are rotting in our plantations. Our cotton and coffee fields are increasingly becoming the subject of a scramble for our crops by the Indians . . .' He paused, and pretended to cough, while studying the faces of his colleagues.

Mutwe-gwa-kyalo was wondering what Tyagiri was actually aiming at. Why not come straight to the point?

'The Chief has told us that everybody is up-to-date with his taxes. We are also happy that our children are bursting the walls of the school. That's a good sign in our village. See how the village booms with a growing number of cattle around it. What else do we lack?'

'What are you trying to say, Father?' asked Mutwe-gwa-kyalo who could no longer contain his suspicions. 'All that you've said is true. But aren't you taking us back to where we started?'

Mutwe-gwa-kyalo had lately sold a piece of land to Tyagiri. There had been a few council-meetings since, but at every one of these meetings Tyagiri had seemed to have changed his former attitude to the Chief. Mutwe-gwa-kyalo thought his man was becoming rather big-headed and un-co-operative with him. It was true that Tyagiri had paid a handsome bit of money for the piece of land, but was it necessary for him to try to play big in a village council? Was Kayonga village, as a whole, not the property of Mutwe-gwa-kyalo, the boss of everybody who lived in it?

'Father,' Tyagiri seemed to read what was passing in the Chief's mind, 'isn't it true that a wise man becomes wiser by borrowing from other people's heads? Isn't it true that a rich man becomes richer through the toils of those he exploits? But is it true that *a* foolish man is always *the* foolish one?'

'Why inundate us with proverbs?' Busungu roared impatiently. 'Who doesn't know them? Why don't you stop circumventing and come to the point?'

'I'm coming to that, Father. Don't eat the flower before the fruit is ripe. Did not our fathers say that one should capture the fox while it salivated? We've succeeded in raising more and better crops because we have pleased our labourers with more pay. But that is still pulling our fox by the tail . . .' Tyagiri paused and swallowed a lump, but immediately he continued.

'Fathers, we have to capture the whole fox. Our herds of cattle are expanding because of the good care given to them by our herdsmen. Why should we not give these men something to please them so that we gain more from them?'

'Ahhhh, now, there you are again,' the council roared, each man expressing his own opinion, laughingly, 'Pay the bushmen in money? . . . Do we have to throw away our money just like that? Hohohoho . . . Money to the savages? . . . They don't need it anyway . . . The more cattle they raise for us, the more milk and butter they get from us . . . Kraalmen have neither feelings nor love for money, brother . . .'

'That's it, Byekwaso,' Tyagiri exclaimed. 'You've got my point, brother. They've no feelings and no love for money. But they *have* feelings and love for cattle. They would feel more secure and happy tending a few of their own cattle among ours.'

Tyagiri stopped and searched their faces. Everyone stared back unbelievingly. Did they hear what he said correctly? Was their brother out of his mind . . .? Then Mutwe-gwa-kyalo asked Tyagiri out of curiosity:

'Father, if I've heard you properly, are you asking us to pay Karekyezi, and all the rest of them, in cattle?'

'I'm not asking anybody to do such a thing, to *pay* in cattle,' replied Tyagiri.

'Are you then suggesting it?'

'No, Father. I'm suggesting something else,' went on Tyagiri, 'Something that won't do any harm, or make any loss, to anyone of those who accept my idea. If it pleases the council, let's *give* Karekyezi a newly-born calf every once in a while . . .'

They all burst out laughing boisterously. Tyagiri had certainly lost his head. What a preposterous idea! That was the trouble, trying to be good to savages. Once they entered into your head they began to eat out your heart and suck your blood. Tyagiri's head was not free!

'Medicine, Fathers, medicine,' Luyombo shouted, 'A bushman's medicine. The savage has charmed our brother. Do they play, these jungle-people? Do you think they

74

smoke only tobacco in their pipes? They smoke their medicines and the winds carry the medicines into the hearts of the people the savages intend to charm, you see? Hohohoho ,they've charmed him . . .'

When everybody had roared with laughter at Luyombo's passionate string of words, Tyagiri spoke again calmly.

'Father, you have the peace to think, believe and shout out whatever grips your imagination. Yes, I'm charmed. But not by Karekyezi's pipe. I'm charmed by the excellent work he has done, and still does, for all of us. Many of you who are laughing, entrusted him with only one cow. Aren't you now boasting of the steers and heifers which you own through this man's hard work?'

Their smiles died on their lips. No one answered his challenge. Then after a pause the Chief commented:

'But I don't see how your suggestion fits in.'

'It *does* fit in, Father.' explained Tyagiri, 'I've not suggested that one gives Karekyezi a calf every time one's cows give birth. I said once in a while, and the calf should be a bull. To them a bull is as good as a cow. He'll love it. It'll increase his fire for hard work.'

'How then can your plan work?' the Chief asked.

'It will work like this. If one of us gives him a baby bull this year, another could do so the next year or the year after. Those of us who have their cattle in other kraals could do the same. Why don't we keep these people happy at our work?'

There was silence again as they digested the matter. Who would do such a thing? Illogical! Karekyezi and the rest of his kind were mere employees. It had never been heard of that a labourer could also pick his master's cotton or coffee for sale for himself. Tyagiri had always said useful things, but not this time.

75

'It may relieve your minds, Fathers, to know that I've already taken the initiative for this year,' Tyagiri reported to the council, 'And I wish any one of you was there to witness what came from this man's heart. You simply can't imagine how they love cattle.'

'But is it an obligation, then?' Lozio asked, 'I mean, will your action not bind the rest of us? Will this man not always expect a calf when our cows give birth?'

'Not at all. It's entirely up to each individual,' said Tyagiri.

Mutwe-gwa-kyalo and the rest of the council sighed with relief.

'Let the fools do it,' the Chief told himself. For he knew that he, personally, would never ever part with a gift to another person. Was he not the one to get gifts from the people of his village? A whole bull to a *mulaalo*? The Chief felt a pang of jealousy gnawing inside him. Tyagiri was thoughtless. Could he not present that bull to his own Chief who had even sold him a piece of land? Was that the way to thank the Chief? How narrow-minded people were! What benefit was Tyagiri going to get from Karekyezi apart from having his cattle grazed like any other cattle? Was Karekyezi going to graze Tyagiri's cattle on special grass dropped from heaven? No, his brother was clearly charmed by the savage's medicine smoked in the pipe . . .

The people of Kayonga village believed that those who smoked pipes not only smoked tobacco in them, but also various kinds of medicines given to them by their consulting witch-doctors. People visited witch-doctors for various reasons and they paid money, goats or snow-white chickens as a fee. Some of these people wanted to be rich; others wanted to settle matters with their enemies, but first they had to soften their hearts before they made peace with them.

There were those who visited a *muganga* – witch-doctor – in order to secure the return of their wives who had eloped with their lovers. Others went to seek a way to win the hearts of the beautiful girls they wanted to marry, especially if those girls showed no interest in such men. Then there were those who were constantly pestered by thieves and wanted to keep them away from their homesteads.

The *muganga* would give them medicines, some of which were mixed with bits and pieces of animal and bird talons, feathers or animal hairs. With these they would get instructions to follow while smoking the charms.

'Never shake anybody's hand especially a woman's hand. Otherwise the power of the charm and your luck will go to that person . . .'

'Stand on the roof of a thatched house twice a day, before sunrise and after sunset, while you pronounce to the four winds your wish to be rich . . .'

'You must squat at the cross-roads once for nine consecutive nights. Each time call your wife by name and one of the roads will bring her back . . .'

'Smoke this medicine while you stand by the headside of an old grave for seven consecutive midnights. Call your lover by her maiden name. Then do whatever you can to see that she eats your food or drinks your *mwenge*. You must drop this dried and crushed piece of flesh from a crocodile's vagina into whichever one she chooses; this will bind her heart to you . . .'

'Woman, smoke this medicine facing the rising sun and pronounce your wish to have a baby. As the sun goes down into its abyss, jump into bed with your husband. That sunset will sink the baby into your womb . . .'

Since the kraals were always in the bush, the people of Kayonga village firmly believed that kraal-people could not be excelled in the making of medicines which could twist anybody's heart to respond to their wishes.

77

Kraalmen's charms, the people of Kayonga said, could madden, scatter leprosy, or even kill!

If kraalmen hated you, the people of Kayonga said, they would smoke their charms and make your cows barren. Many of those who believed this tried to make friends with kraalmen simply for the safety of their own homesteads and of their cattle. They believed that the pungent smell of kraalmen's tobacco could plunge the whole village into the clutches of pestilence!

As the people of Kayonga village never marked their bodies, they always looked at Karekyezi's tattoos with mixed feelings. They thought they were a sign of powerful influences against ferocious beasts and other enemies incised into his body. Even a lion, these people said, would hide in a bush when it smelled Karekyezi's presence!

Kabahuma and her husband were not aware of the beliefs of people in Kayonga village. They and their family lived in a world of their own – the world of seclusion, the world of outcasts.

TEN

WHATEVER influence this council meeting might have had on the minds of the cattle-owners of Kayonga village, it made very little, or no difference at all, to Karekyezi. Every calving season had meant a growth in the size of his own stock, and now his mind was set for leaving the service.

His few benefactors included Lozio who had fed Karekyezi and his family more than any other employer in the village. But even Lozio had to lose a few baby cows to Karekyezi like anybody else since he was still one of the village bunch who could not use their heads properly.

Now that his mind was made up Karekyezi's behaviour towards his employers began to change. Leaving the cattle in the charge of his juniors he went to visit Rweza and the other relatives who looked after his stolen cattle. He spent more than a month in the hills that lay several rivers away from Kayonga village. During this time he went from ridge to ridge, notifying his kinsmen of his intention to join them now that he had accumulated enough cattle to fit into their community. He was now rich and would look forward to more cattle coming in from those kinsmen still in the employment of the stupid village people.

He made use of the time to take a good rest; he had not had one since he started herding the village people's cattle as a young man. His people welcomed him with *mwenge* they bought from the surrounding villages and

Karekyezi felt completely shed of his responsibility to the Kayonga villagers. It was not that he rarely visited his relatives; he would go and stay with them for a couple of days or so to celebrate with them after he had sent in new calves. Whenever he made such visits he always left instructions with Kabahuma to send for him should anything happen during his absence. This time Karekyezi had left instructions that she should *not* contact him.

'I have a lot of work to do there,' he told her, 'If they ask for me tell them anything sensible . . . and sell plenty of milk, we may need the money. Take care of everything; the boys are big enough to protect the kraal and the cattle in the pastures . . .'

'Is it time then?' Kabahuma asked her husband.

'Yes, our people are waiting to help me build our own kraal among them,' Karekyezi replied.

'Then go with God's blessing. I'll take care of everything; don't you know your Kabahuma?'

Karekyezi left before dawn so that he could catch up with his people before they took their cattle to the pastures. Some days went by with life in his kraal under the full control of his wife, but it was not long after Karekyezi's departure that the people of Kayonga village began to feel his absence. Many of his employers began to get less and less milk; those who had few cattle got no milk at all. When they asked Kabahuma what had happened, she only told them that their cows did not give enough milk even to suckle their calves.

'Don't the cows eat enough grass?' they would ask.

'They do', Kabahuma would reply, 'so what can we do about it?'

'Where's Karekyezi, anyway?' they persisted.

'He went to see our sick people and to bury those who are dying,' lied Kabahuma. 'Lord-of-mine, it's terrible what's happening among our people . . .'

As the days went by Kabahuma got more and more queries from the people of Kayonga village.

'When do you expect him back then?' they asked.

'Lord-of-mine,' Kabahuma would retort, 'death doesn't tell when it'll stop taking our people. I don't know when he'll come back.'

Karekyezi's employers began to get impatient. They approached Mutwe-gwa-kyalo about the matter, and this prompted the Chief himself to go to the kraal to speak to Kabahuma. He, Tyagiri and Lozio were among the very few who still got their daily supplies of milk. When he had found Kabahuma he immediately came to the point.

'This is going too far, Kabahuma,' he told her. 'You must see to it that these people get their milk. This dying of your people has got nothing to do with the welfare of my people. Send for your husband to return immediately and report to me.'

'But, lord-of-mine,' Kabahuma replied, 'our people are so many, and scattered all over the country, that I don't know where to contact him. But I'll try.'

Kabahuma, however, only sent a message to let Karekyezi know the lie of the land.

Whatever was happening at home, Karekyezi told his kinsmen when he received the message, that the situation was well under control – Kabahuma was a wonderful woman. And with this thought in mind Karekyezi stayed on until the erection of his new kraal was completed.

'When shall we see you then, Karekyezi?' his relatives asked as he left for Kayonga village.

'As you all know these people, I don't think it will be long,' he replied. 'And I don't care what they say or do; our Kabahuma and the children will soon be here.'

On his way home Karekyezi suddenly decided to visit one of the kraals on the outskirts of Kayonga village. As luck would have it, he found his friends singing and dancing together. They were enjoying themselves from a large calabash of *mwenge* they had bought in the village.

'Whatever have you been doing, Karekyezi?' they called to him. 'Working on young brides while your masters are shouting for their milk?'

'Pthoooh, ahiiiiima, *kaate*,' Karekyezi replied without concern. 'Let them milk their wives if they want milk. Forget about them and hand me the gourd.'

'Ahiii, Karekyezi, what's got into your head?' they asked. 'The last one you slept with must have eaten your heart. You think if those people hear what you say they won't sack you?'

'I'm not like you who are afraid of being sacked,' he replied, 'I've used my head long enough now. And if you want to know, my own kraal is ready. That is where I have been during the whole moon.'

'What? What?' every one of them asked eagerly. 'Have you already a good number to start the new life?'

'A good number?' Karekyezi roared with laughter. 'Do you call a hundred a good number or a rich number?'

'A hundred? A hundred! Pheeew,' they all thundered, whistling long and loud. 'Where are we then? What are we doing?'

'Still playing between your wives' legs and forgetting to use your heads,' Karekyezi retorted as he gulped eagerly from the gourd and again roared with laughter.

He repeated the same old advice and the principles on which he had based his practical undertakings enabling him to set himself and his family free from the slavery of the people who discriminated against them; the people who saw them as uncivilized savages, the outcasts. As the party went on, Karekyezi continued with his sermon making a deep impression on his friends' minds. They knew now what they would do and soon they expected to get more cattle into their kraals. Would not the owners invite them to take all those Karekyezi was going to leave? They were happy and stimulated at the prospect.

Karekyezi was a little intoxicated when he left for his own kraal late in the afternoon; he went along the way singing and jumping in a solo dance. Then he met one of the people of Kayonga village who stopped to talk to him.

'Karekyezi, when did you come back?'

'Why, I'm just on my way back now,' he replied.

'Your wife hasn't been giving me milk for the last three Sundays,' he complained. 'Why was that?'

'You make me laugh, Father, do you expect Kabahuma to produce milk like a cow?' replied Karekyezi carelessly.

He went on singing and jumping and the man stared, he was badly hit by the unexpected answer from this savage. How dare Karekyezi give such an answer to a person who employed him, who gave him and his family their life?

'Karekyezi, is that the way to answer your masters or are you trying to insult me?' asked the man angrily.

'I'm not insulting you, I'm answering your question, Father,' returned Karekyezi.

'We'll see what the Chief says about your behaviour, you fool,' the man concluded.

Karekyezi moved on, singing to himself and dancing. Before he reached the way branching off to his kraal he met another man who asked him a similar question about the milk. Karekyezi eyed the man, jumped up and down again singing, and then answered him.

'But what's the matter with everybody, Father? Must my bride Kabahuma take the blame when the cows do not give enough milk?'

'It's you who is to blame, Karekyezi,' he said, 'because the cows have not been properly grazed during your self-granted absence. And how can you sing so joyfully and

83

dance if your people have been dying like flies? I should say that you've been drinking only, keeping away from your duty.'

'Let me ask you this, Father,' said Karekyezi, 'do you think that when I'm here to look after the cows I put the grass into their mouths? If they don't have enough milk, is it my fault?'

'It certainly *is* your fault, you savage,' retorted the man.

Karekyezi kept silent for a long time studying the man's face. He held his long grazing stick, his companion-at-arms, which he never left behind. Karekyezi thought of using it now that he did not care about the consequences, but on second thoughts he controlled himself and paid the man back in his own coin.

'Do you expect me to milk Kabahuma's teats or my penis to get enough milk for people to drink?' he shouted.

The man was livid with anger. Flames of hatred leaped into his eyes. He clenched his fists ready to attack, but then saw that Karekyezi was slowly raising his stick. Fuming with rage, he thought of springing at Karekyezi and strangling him to death. Karekyezi's stick, however, was slowly reaching a level from where it could not miss its target; the man changed his mind and walked swiftly to the Chief's home. Karekyezi went on to his kraal whistling merrily.

'My beautiful one,' he called to Kabahuma, when he arrived 'are you there?'

'Ayiyiyi, my husband, is it you I'm seeing . . .?' she greeted him. 'Ayiyiyi, welcome home. Has everything gone well with you there?'

'Everything has gone well there . . . until I met those people who insulted me in the village?' Karekyezi replied.

'What has happened, husband-of-mine?'

'I've told them, I've told everybody, to leave you

alone,' he exclaimed. 'They say you don't give them milk; I say my bride doesn't produce milk like a cow. Another one says it's my fault that they don't get their milk. I asked him if I should milk your teats or my penis . . .'

'Aweee, did you say that, really?' Kabahuma, who had started to simper, suddenly became serious, 'With the same words?'

'Exactly so,' Karekyezi replied defiantly. 'I was even ready to beat one of them but he feared my stick. I would have beaten him up if he had dared lay his hands on me.'

'But when you're drunk, as I see you are, why don't you remember that they're your masters? . . . and where have you been drinking?' asked Kabahuma.

'I've been drinking at Mutabaruka's kraal and what you say may be right. But how can they be my masters any more when we are going, leaving them once and for all? Do you think we shall stay here after what has happened between me and their brothers? I tell you, you had better pack up and be ready to go at any time from now.'

When the boys brought back the cattle, Karekyezi repeated the story to them, told them what was awaiting them in the fertile hills where their new home was.

'Of course, some of you will have to come back into these villages to look for jobs. Like you, Barigye. You're big enough to look after cattle and bring us some more. And when Kagabu's time comes he will do the same. Don't think I have gathered these animals for you.'

That night was a busy one in the kraal. Karekyezi moved about among the cattle, wishing them goodbye, for he had already suspected what would be the outcome of his earlier confrontation with the village people. He knew that the council would be called for his dismissal any time.

The following morning Karekyezi and his group had

just finished milking the cows when Tyagiri and Lozio arrived. Their faces were serious and Tyagiri's words were hard.

'You're the most stupid person we've ever seen,' he bawled at Karekyezi. 'My friend here and I have been trying for a long time to help you and your family. We gave you calves to make you happy. Now see what you've done for yourself. How can you insult the people who keep you alive with their milk?'

'Lord-of-mine,' Karekyezi pretended to be sorry, 'I was only drunk if I made anybody angry. I only ask them to excuse me . . .'

'There's no excuse, Karekyezi,' Tyagiri went on. 'Drunkards do not flay dogs, but you have. The council is already meeting and both of us felt too ashamed to be there. Your fellow *balaalo* were notified last evening to take over all the cattle in this kraal today. So you see we can't help you any more . . .'

'Then what shall I do if the cattle are taken away from me?' asked Karekyezi.

'You can do nothing,' Lozio told him. 'You have lost all chance of ever having your own cattle. Now look, they're all coming. Do you still think you have a chance?'

Mutwe-gwa-kyalo was leading a group of cattle-owners who came with their kettles to collect the milk. Along with them came a group of kraalmen, some of whom had been with Karekyezi the evening before. The Chief spoke straight to Tyagiri and Lozio.

'Fathers,' he said, 'Your absence at the meeting has helped a great deal to ease the matter. Our arrival here puts this man out of his job with immediate effect. Every one of us has come to point out his cattle to the new *balaalo* from the other kraals. Do you have anything to say, Fathers?'

'Suppose we two, and perhaps other owners also, still want this man to keep our cattle for us, Father?' Tyagiri asked carefully, almost knowing the answer.

'You can do so, Fathers. That's entirely up to you,' replied the Chief. 'But not here in my village and not anywhere *near* my land. I know that you have your own land, Father, but that land is still on Kayonga village where all the insulted people live.'

Mutwe-gwa-kyalo did not wait for more arguments. He ordered the cattle-owners to sort out their animals and hand them over to whichever *mulaalo* they chose from the group they had brought along with them. Tyagiri and Lozio had no alternative; they had to obey the wish of the majority, for it was only their cattle which now remained. They handed them to Mutabaruka.

'Bring out all the milk you've taken this morning!' the Chief ordered Karekyezi who looked very sad when the cattle were taken away.

After what looked like a Milk Harvest ceremony, the people began to disperse with full kettles, the cattle, mooing, were driven off in different directions. One of the people who had been insulted by Karekyezi turned and shouted.

'Now you can go and milk your tail for your own milk to drink . . .'

'Aweee,' Kabahuma exclaimed, 'this man is shameless!'

Karekyezi looked at his two young calves, then at his younger brothers and the children and burst out into a boisterous laughter. He laughed and laughed. Tears rolled down his face; he held the sides of his chest, squeezed his stomach, and sat down in the *saazi*.

'Kabahuma,' he called, still roaring and clutching his abdomen, 'hasn't it come true that when a maker shapes a spear he never imagines that one day it might

87

stab him? Hohohoho, maweee, awuuu, *kaate rubura,* pthoooh. Now they have it in the back!'

Kabahuma joined in the laughter. Then everybody joined in; even the children, who did not understand the significance of the proverb, burst out into giggles. For them it was fun to see Karekyezi clutching his stomach and roaring with laughter, tears running down his face.

'Outcasts, they call us. Yohohoho. Who has ever heard of rich outcasts? Yohohoho, awuu, awuuu . . . *kaate rubura* . . . pthoooh . . . *nyabura nyowe* . . ahiiiiiiima,' he roared.